GREASE
TOWN

GREASE TOWN

ANN TOWELL

TUNDRA BOOKS

Text copyright © 2010 by Ann Towell

Published in Canada by Tundra Books,
75 Sherbourne Street, Toronto, Ontario M5A 2P9

Published in the United States by Tundra Books of Northern New York,
P.O. Box 1030, Plattsburgh, New York 12901

Library of Congress Control Number: 2009941215

Library and Archives Canada Cataloguing in Publication

Towell, Ann
Grease town / Ann Towell.

For ages 10-14.
ISBN 978-0-88776-983-2

I. Title.

PS8589.O93G74 2010 jC813'.54 C2009-906906-7

We acknowledge the financial support of the Government of Canada
through the Book Publishing Industry Development Program (BPIDP) and
that of the Government of Ontario through the Ontario Media
Development Corporationís Ontario Book Initiative. We further acknowledge
the support of the Canada Council for the Arts and the Ontario Arts Council
for our publishing program. ONTARIO ARTS COUNCIL
CONSEIL DES ARTS DE L'ONTARIO

Design: Leah Springate
Printed and bound in Canada

This book is printed on ancient-forest friendly paper.

1 2 3 4 5 6   15 14 13 12 11 10

In loving memory of my parents,
Hermannus and Antonia Dekker.

CHAPTER

I

I live in a swamp. A dirty mess that reeks of sulphur and oozes black liquid that everyone says is as precious as gold. The squeal of wooden wagon wheels, the steady thump of the springboards, the creaking of the jerker lines and the squeaking hand pumps are the rhythm for all who work there.

The men don't talk much when they work. Theirs is the kind of silence that makes you think everything is all right, but it's only men's excitement simmering under the surface like a pot before it starts to boil. Sometimes you don't see the bubbles until it's too late.

My friend, Moses, said his father walked miles to this country, only to move from one swamp to another. It just doesn't make sense he told me, his eyes laughing along with his mouth. His pa came from the state of

Mississippi in the United States of America. He's happy here because he's free.

"It's that simple," Moses said. "Freedom is happiness. Don't matter if you're rich or poor, just as long as you're free."

I believe that because Moses is a lot smarter than me. But he doesn't come into this story until later. He's one of the reasons I've stopped talking. There are others, but I'll tell them as they come up.

I lived with my Aunt Sadie after my parents died. You see, Aunt Sadie's sister married my Uncle Amos's brother. That sister and that brother were my ma and pa. For six long months I lived with Aunt Sophie, trying to please her. She only had rules about things that didn't matter much. I finally ran away with my brother, Lemuel, to Uncle Amos's house.

I should probably tell you first, how I came about living in this swamp. My pa and ma both died from the fevers. Pa's brother, Uncle Amos, was a doctor then and tried to save my folks, but he couldn't. Aunt Sadie figured God needed Ma and Pa more than we did, so He came and took them. I pictured his big hand coming out of the sky and plucking them out of their beds. That big hand was in my nightmares for a long time.

It wasn't so bad living with Aunt Sadie during the week when most of my days were spent away from her, at school. But come the weekend, she was unbearable. I was constantly being nagged to pick up after myself. I was afraid to even sit on the chairs in case one broke right out from under me.

It made me miss my parents even more. Sometimes I'd cry at night to the sound of the left-over crickets that didn't have sense enough to see that the frost would kill them too. My heart was sore and feeling broken with loneliness.

Lemuel kept busy working as an apprentice for a blacksmith. He lived near the forge and hardly came to visit me. He's six years older than me, so that would make him nineteen years old.

Well, one day when he did come to see me, he told us he was tired of his job. He was going to Uncle Amos's place in the Enniskillen swamp because they had just discovered oil there. I was excited and sad at the same time – excited for him and sad for me.

He was going to buy some draught horses and work as a teamster, driving the heavy wagons holding barrels filled with oil. I asked him if I could go with him, even though I felt Aunt Sadie's eyes on me, like daggers. Lem ignored me.

Aunt Sadie sat very straight in her chair as if her shoulders were glued to the back of it. "Where will you take the oil?" she asked, disapproval written all over her face.

"I plan on carting it to the refineries." Lemuel took a sip of the tea with a wry face and looked at my uncle, Robert, who up until now had been sitting quietly. He is a banker and very successful. The brick house they live in is nice with lace curtains. The girl, Mary, does all the heavy chores so my aunt can spend time visiting and doing her church work.

Uncle Robert knew about the refineries in Sarnia, and he and Lem talked for a while. I lost track of their conversation because I was thinking how awful life was going to be once my brother left.

The next day at school, my friend Eli said to me, real serious like, "If I was you, I'd run away."

I answered him just as quick, "Can I move in with you?"

Eli looked surprised. "No, I don't figure you can. My ma has enough kids, and I don't suppose she needs another."

"Where should I go then? I suppose when you run, you need a place to run to."

We both sat under a tree. He was chewing on a blade of grass. "Run away with Lem, dummy!"

"Lem won't take me with him," I said. "He knows I'm supposed to stay here and finish school."

"I'd go if I could," he remarked, spitting the grass out of his mouth. Eli reads a lot of adventure stories, and I think he was pretending one, through me.

"Why *don't* you go?" I asked in a cross voice. "You know there'd be the devil to pay."

Eli looked at the ground then back up at me. "I guess the problem is you're just too scared."

This made me very angry even though Eli watched out for me during school. Often the boys would play "keep away" with my glasses, or they would push me around until Eli came to the rescue.

Eli could see that I was getting worked up, and that's what he wanted. "Just think of how everyone here will look up to you if you go."

That did get me thinking. I was tired of being the whipping boy of the classroom. It'd be a nice to have my classmates respect me, for a change.

The day before my brother was to leave, some boys got a hold of my hat and were tossing it around between them. Eli finally came up behind one of them and boxed his ears. He took the hat back.

"See what I mean?" he said, handing the hat to me. "You'd get respect."

Well, sir, that's when I decided I'd stow away on my brother's wagon.

The rest of that night I planned how I would do it. Lem stayed with us the Friday night before he left. He'd wanted to leave on Sunday, but Aunt Sadie carried on about "honoring the Sabbath," so he decided to leave on Saturday, instead. I needed to get up very early, before he did, in order to succeed.

Aunt Sadie's Mary prepared a really special meal for us. I was silent at suppertime, and I caught Aunt Sadie watching me more than once. I looked down so she couldn't see my eyes. Aunt Sadie says that the eyes are the mirror of the soul. Well, this was one soul she wasn't going to see.

Later, I hid my clothes under some sacking Lemuel had put in the back to protect his own belongings. I hoped he wouldn't notice mine. My own dog-eared copy of *Moby Dick* lay under the burlap too. I figured I might want to read it again. I came back into the house, whistling as if I hadn't a care in the world.

"You should get to bed early so you can see your

brother off tomorrow," Aunt Sadie said, putting the meat platter carefully onto the sideboard.

"Yes ma'am, but I would like to spend a bit more time with him now, if I could," Her eyes softened toward me.

"You can stay up for another half hour. Then off to bed with you."

I sat on the floor beside my brother listening to everything he said. I especially wanted to know what time he was leaving, so I could hide on the wagon.

"I'm not sure how Amos will take to having you there, Lem. He's not known to be sociable," Uncle Robert said. He tamped the tobacco down into his pipe. He took a piece of kindling and stuck it in the fire. Then he lit his pipe and stared at the flames as if mesmerized. "I dare say it'll take some getting used to living down there. But," he sighed, "nothing ventured, nothing gained."

"What do you mean?" I asked.

"It's a manner of speaking, boy, a figure of speech."

"Oh," I whispered. I wanted to ask so many questions, but knew this wasn't the time for interrupting. I sat quiet until summoned for bed.

That night my body seemed too small to contain all the excitement rolled up in my stomach. I lay still on the bed to stop the dizziness. I heard the rest of them say goodnight and Lemuel walk down the hall to the guest room, which was next to mine.

It was a long while before I drifted off to sleep. I heard the creak of Lemuel's bed. He got up a few times in the night too. I guess he was as nervous as me. I hoped he wouldn't be too angry when he discovered I was with him tomorrow.

"Titus, get on down here!" Aunt Sadie's call woke me up.

I came down to a breakfast of steaming porridge and even coffee for all of us. I gobbled my food and watched my brother do the same. He was in an all-fired rush to get out of there, before the roads got crowded with oxen carts carrying vegetables and fruit from the country into town.

We all went outside and stood in front of the house, the house with the lace curtains at the windows. I couldn't seem to find a way to sneak onto the wagon without anyone noticing. I asked if I could ride with Lem a ways to say a last good-bye.

At first, Aunt Sadie said no and told me I needed to weed the front gardens for her. But Uncle Robert was on my side.

"Let the boy go, Sadie. It's just for a bit. He'll be back soon to help out here."

Aunt Sadie gave in. I hopped onto the seat of the wagon, next to my brother, and tried not to smile too widely. Uncle Robert hit the rump of one horse and the team started moving slowly down the street. Lemuel glanced back once, waving enthusiastically. Then he threw his hat in the air and whooped. I didn't mind getting down to fetch it for him.

He waited until I got back on. Then he started in on me. "Mind Aunt Sadie now, you hear? When I get settled there, I'll send for you."

"Why can't I go now and help you get settled?"

"It isn't fittin'. You've got school first. Besides, you're just a kid."

He turned in his seat, but kept his hands steady on the reins. "It's a man's world where I'm goin', Titus, and you won't like it. Ma wanted you to finish school and go to college." He paused. "You know that."

"I'm getting bigger, Lemuel. I already read hard books. The teacher said I'm almost ready for normal school."

"Ma wanted you to stay in, and I mean to see that you do by leaving you with Aunt Sadie."

"You're doing nothin' of the sort. You're just running off on an adventure and leaving me alone."

I jumped off of the wagon, landing in the dust of the road. It puffed up around me, like powder, making my trousers all dirty.

"You'll write me won't you? I want to hear about everything." I said.

Lem got off of the wagon and hugged me hard enough to almost break my back.

"I love you, Titus, and don't forget it. I'm just trying to make my way in the world. I'll send for you when I'm ready."

I pretended to forgive him and hugged him back. I started for home, while he got back up on the wagon. The farmers were coming into town already. Lemuel was preoccupied, keeping his team in line, while he waited for the road to clear. He didn't notice me sneak onto his wagon.

I know I've been rambling a bit, but I need the story to come out right somehow.

There are times you just want to lay your burden down. But this is mostly about Moses's burden, not mine. I cared for him like a brother, though it wouldn't seem like it in the end because when push came to shove, there was nothing I could do to help him.

CHAPTER

2

I was under the sacking. The dust was tickling my
nose. I hoped I wouldn't sneeze. I didn't want Lemuel
to find me until I was good and ready to be found. We
were on the road for quite a while, and I must have
drifted off to sleep because I awoke with a jolt.

The wagon was running over something that tossed
it around like a ship at sea. I thought of *Moby Dick* and
remembered Ishmael listening to Father Mapple's
sermon, about the disobedient Jonah who goes on a
ship fleeing from God. I was like him, fleeing from God
– and Aunt Sadie.

I inched my way to the end of the wagon. I peered
out from under the burlap and saw what was making
the trip so rough. The road was made out of logs. We
were on a corduroy road. I felt a little sick from the
uneven movement of the wagon, not to mention my

aching backside. I closed my eyes to stop myself from feeling worse.

My mind trembled and I was struck with my own wickedness. I'd run away and made Aunt Sadie worry, and now, Lemuel would be angry too. I wondered if I should have come out from hiding right then to face the storm that was surely brewing.

But no, sir. Now you see my true character. I would rather wait to show myself; wait until we were so far from London that Lemuel would *have* to take me with him; wait until Aunt Sadie paced the floor in worry. I felt guilty, but not guilty enough. I had come too far to go back. It was like the oil fever had gotten a strangle hold of me too.

I sniffled and felt sorry for myself, but only for a short while. I felt a little better when the sun's friendly warmth heated up the sacking. Lemuel was whistling on the front seat and the wagon was still tipping and swaying along the road. I knew I would have bruises all over my body by the time we reached wherever we were going.

Patience is not my strong virtue. I used to talk too much, and I don't listen very well to others. I wanted so badly to come out from under the sacking. My legs were itching with the thought of moving my body, but I kept telling myself to lie still. I didn't want to be sent back.

The dull sound of the wind in the trees accompanied us all that day. Despite the jerking motion of the wagon and the clop clopping of the horses, I fell asleep again. I woke up when the wagon came to a standstill. I didn't dare move. I could hear the clomp of boots as Lemuel got down. He called out to someone, asking if he could water the horses. There were other voices nearby. The wagon jolted as the horses moved to a trough to drink. The slurping and sloshing of water made me very thirsty.

Lemuel wandered off and so did the others. I waited a while, unsure of what to do. But Lemuel was gone for so long, I couldn't resist moving out from under the sack. I lifted my head and then slowly inched my way to look over the side of the wagon. A strong hand clamped down on my collar and lifted me up. My heart slipped down to the bottom of my shoes. I could hardly breathe. My collar was cutting off my windpipe. I kicked my feet, hoping to defend myself.

"What have we here? Hey fellers lookee here. I got me a stowaway!" He had already put me on the ground, but didn't let go.

"Let the boy go." A second man was fastening the bridle on his horse.

They talked kind of funny. I know now that they spoke like southerners, like butter wouldn't melt in their mouths.

The man by the horse said, "You're cutting off the boy's air. He can scarcely breathe."

The hand loosened its grip. "Come here, lad," the bridle-tightening man beckoned.

You could tell he was what Aunt Sadie called "quality" by the way he was dressed. His clothes were finer than usual. His coat lifted a little in the breeze, and I saw a gun in a holster on his hip.

"Now . . . you must have a good reason for being on this wagon." His voice rose at the end of his statement making it seem like a question.

"Well sir," my gaze faltered, and I mumbled something in my fear. My glasses were crooked and dirty, and I wanted to fix them, but didn't dare do anything.

"Speak up boy," he said, sterner this time.

"It's my brother's wagon," I said. The man bent down so he could hear me. "He's in there." I pointed toward the two-storey frame inn.

"Your brother?"

"Yes sir," I nodded trying to be very polite. I hoped Lemuel would come out soon and rescue me.

"Come along then, and you point out your brother to me."

I followed him into the building and the other man followed. There were long tables stretched across the room. One woman stood behind a counter and was serving up something that looked like stew. I realized how hungry, how dusty, how lonely I was.

Lemuel had his head down, scooping the food into his mouth as if he didn't have a moment to spare. He didn't look up until we bumped against his table. He noticed the gentleman first. He stood up in a mannerly way and finally caught sight of me, trying to hide behind the man. Lem's eyes widened and his eyebrows came down in a scowl.

"Where did you come from?" he growled at me.

The gentleman spoke, "It's obvious you know who this young scamp is."

"Yes sir, I do. And you have the right of it, calling him a scamp."

"He claims he's your brother."

"He is that, sir."

"Well, I'll leave him to you then. Good day."

Lemuel nodded his head, then he turned to me. His eyes were like the hot coals of the smithy.

"How did you end up here? I don't suppose you ran all the way behind the wagon?"

"No," I mumbled. "I rode on the back of the wagon under the sacking. You're not sending me back though, are you Lemuel? I can help you with the horses and cooking and everything. I won't be a bother. I promise. Just don't send me back." My hands were clutching at his coat.

"Sit down. Quit making a spectacle of yourself. You might as well eat. I've got some serious thinking to do." He called to the woman to bring another bowl of stew with some bread.

She came with it, the steam rising. I didn't dare say anything while Lemuel appeared to be thinking. He mopped up the gravy with the heel of his bread. He must have been as hungry as I was.

While Lem was thinking about what to do with me, the people at the next table talked about the man with the gun. They figured he was a bounty hunter because he was asking questions about an escaped slave. He had a reward poster with a drawing on it, but no one in these parts had seen the slave.

The man who had grabbed me by the collar was sitting in the corner of the room eyeing us carefully. I didn't trust him. There was just something about his eyes that didn't sit right with me.

He had a huge mug of beer in front of him and took a swallow as I watched. He smacked his lips in an exaggerated manner and wiped his mouth with the back of his hand. Then he laughed, and I shivered in spite of myself.

The woman came to be paid for the food and Lem pulled a little money sack out of his pocket. I heard the scrape of a chair being pushed back, along the floor. Without looking, I knew it was that man. I heard the heavy trudge of feet coming our way and hoped they would keep walking right past us and out the door.

Lemuel looked up at someone behind me and asked, "Can I help you?"

"Where you headed?"

Lemuel hesitated, "Enniskillen Township."

"The oil fields?"

Lem's eyes flashed, "How did you know?"

"Nothing else worth anything in those swamplands."

"Well I guess we should push off. Come on, Titus."

"Wait a minute, mister. I could make it worth your while if you were to take me with you," the stranger said. "Us miners need to stick together."

The man took a small pouch out of his pocket, much like the one Lemuel had. "This here is filled with money. I'll pay you twenty dollars to take me with you. My horse died just last week and I can't find another in these here parts."

He took off his hat and put it over his heart as if he was mourning the death of his horse, and maybe he was. Some men like their animals better than people. It's a known fact. I've seen it often enough since moving here.

When Lem still hesitated, the man said, "It's a princely sum."

"Well I figure twenty dollars is a good sum. I could take you for that, mister. The name's Lemuel Sullivan, and this here is my brother, Titus."

"An Irishman, eh? The name's John Longville." He reached out his hand to shake.

"How long do you figure before we get there?" Lemuel asked.

"Well . . . if the rain holds off, another day or so. Once she rains, the road is mucky and mean."

So we left that place, and we had us a traveling partner. John and Lem hit it off at the beginning, but me, I never trusted him. I had the welt on my neck to prove he was a mean-tempered man.

CHAPTER

3

I was glad to be out in the open. I never saw such beautiful maples. When we drove under them, I felt totally covered in yellow light.

We were still on that corduroy road and my backside could attest to that. So far the rain was holding off. Lemuel and John Longville were talking up front. Lem said I was supposed to call him Mister Longville because of the difference in our ages. When I refused, John Longville looked at me, mean-like.

Then he smiled, "Why, the boy can call me John, just like everyone else does. I was never one to put on airs."

Who was he kidding? There didn't seem much about him that was honest and true. He never looked either Lemuel or me straight in the eye when he spoke.

Sometimes I wonder how Lemuel and me can be brothers. He is trusting while I am suspicious of everyone. Lemuel is strong and handsome. I am down-right puny next to him.

Uncle Amos tells me to be patient. "A man in the making takes time," he says, patting me on the head like a puppy dog. But I don't really mind being patted like that by him. He doesn't mean to put me down by it.

John talked about the oil fields and some friends of his there. He said he had been to Enniskillen, but I found out different when we got to Oil Springs. Only one man knew him and his name was Max McQuarrie. Longville got talking about the gold rush in California and said he had been there too. Whether that's true or not is anyone's guess. I, myself, don't believe him. He's what Aunt Sadie would call a veritable blatherskite.

It made me smile to think of her. She has a sharp tongue and uses it regularly, but it's only now I appreciate that in her because she's nowhere near me. Living with her and thinking of her are two very different things.

We passed tollbooths, and the money always came out of Lemuel's pocket. Not once did John open up his pouch to help out. He brought it out of his pocket now and then to shift it from one hand to the other. It jingled as if to remind us of our payment when we would finally be rid of him. I was going write *reward* instead of *payment*, but Uncle Amos said that it wasn't like we were doing something above and beyond just being neighborly. At that time, I thought we were saints to take him with us. Now I know better. We weren't no saints. We were so wrong to bring him to Oil Springs.

While Lem and John were getting friendly we got farther into the country. I was angry that John and Lem got to sit up front, and I got stuck rolling around in the back of the wagon. Lem seemed impressed with all John's stories but I wasn't. They were just stories to my way of thinking.

It started to rain in earnest. There was no way we were going to keep ourselves dry. My clothes were soaked in a matter of minutes, and my teeth began to chatter. I could hardly see through my wet glasses. I suppose we could have sat under the wagon, but the ground was wet too, and surely getting muddier by the minute.

John kept talking even though his hat drooped around his ears, dripping rain onto his hunched shoulders. Finally, the rain was enough, even for his constant talking. The sky was getting darker, and a few times thunder rumbled. There were so many trees you couldn't see the lightning, only the effects of it. The trees flared off and on while the sky danced a merry jig with the storm clouds.

We weren't on a corduroy road anymore. The horses' strength was flagging with the heavy work of pulling us through all the mud. Lemuel shouted for us all to get down off of the wagon. John wanted to stay on and said as much.

"I'll hold the reins and guide them," he suggested hopefully.

"Get down!" Lemuel yelled at him and me. I scrambled off as fast as I could.

"I'm holding the reins. See?" He held them up to John's face only inches from his own. I guess he had had enough of all that talk, and his anger was getting the better of him.

Lemuel led the horses down the road while we walked alongside. The mud grabbed at our boots like slippery hands. The slurp with each step sounded eerie in the approaching darkness. We were all getting tired when the back wheels bogged down in the muck. All the straining with the horses couldn't get us out. Lemuel cut down a sapling and we tried to use it as a lever to free the wheels of the muck. Nothing worked, and it was getting very dark.

I asked Lem if I should maybe light the lamps he'd rigged up on the front of the wagon so we could see better. I was looking under the sacking for the matches, when I heard John holler.

He'd noticed lights up ahead. "Praise be!" He took the hat off of his head and whacked it on his leg. Water sprayed off of it and into my face. I sputtered, but he didn't seem to notice.

He laughed. "I'm heading up to that house. I'll come back with help to get the wagon out."

Well, I'll tell you, Lemuel and me waited there a long time. Drops fell from the leaves above, though it had stopped raining. The air was still, except for the steady drip, drip. The quiet around us was sometimes pierced by the wail of a wild animal. Once it was an unearthly scream we heard and I stepped closer to my brother who was sitting on the end of the wagon. He put his arm around my shoulders and never made fun of me because I was scared.

"It's probably a rabbit caught in a snare." I could tell he was trying to calm me by acting so matter-of-fact about the eerie sounds. Mist could be seen in the shrouded light ahead.

Being so soggy you could just lie down and cry is an awful feeling. I don't think I'd ever been so miserable and cold, except, of course, the day we buried my parents. I could tell Lemuel was getting impatient.

"Now, where in heck did John get to?" he asked himself out loud.

Then he apologized. "I know I shouldn't have said that, but I'm real angry right now."

"I heard that word before, don't worry none about me," I was trying to act worldly as if foul language was a part of my everyday life, though Aunt Sadie would've washed my mouth out with soap if she'd heard me use such words. If only I knew then what I do now, the different kind of words that can come out of a man's mouth. Bitter, nasty words that can lead to violence.

Lemuel wasn't stupid. He knew how Ma and Aunt Sadie had raised us – "I'm used to working around men, and the word just slipped out. I'm really sorry, Titus." He roughed up my hair a bit and then laughed. "May as well unhitch the horses and take them up to where the light is coming from."

Our fingers were cold and damp. Lem fumbled with the leather straps and buckles, while I unhooked one of the lamps and held it high, so he could see what he was doing. Finally, we got the harness all undone. Then the four of us went toward the light.

There was a house with a barn out back where we hoped to bed down the horses for the night. We also hoped the folks who lived there would take kindly to having strangers as houseguests.

There was no use telling me rain was better than snow for if it had snowed, we wouldn't have been in the rut we were in. Winter was always better for traveling. These muddy roads in the country were a colossal nuisance, as Aunt Sadie would say. I had to get Uncle Amos to help me spell that because it had me stumped. He sometimes laughs at the way I spell words, but he's willing to spend time helping me get them right when I ask.

Uncle Amos is good that way. He has always had lots of patience, except when I used to talk too much. That was when I first moved in with him and I talked his "blamed ear off." He said words were supposed to be used for more important things than being irritating.

He sat me down one day and said real solemn-like, "Boy, you got to like yourself. Cause if you don't, no one else will. Talking is just covering up something you don't like. Once your tongue stops wagging, you'll be able to hear yourself think and know what you believe. If you like what you hear in that ol' gob of yours, why then, you'll like yourself." He gave me a quick rap on the head to emphasize his point. I don't think he knew that my feelings were hurt. But now that I can sit back and think, I figure he was right.

But there was a time went Uncle Amos talked too much, too. That was when he was in his cups, as Aunt Sadie would say. He could tell a tall tale at those times and I heard some of them when I lived with him.

Uncle Amos is a teamster, though he was trained to be a doctor. Lem told me that Uncle Amos was part of the Seminole wars down in Florida. He was a doctor in the military. What he saw being done to the Indians he don't talk about much, but it was enough to make him turn against mankind. He was heartily sick of it all, so he moved out of the United States of America and came to Canada.

When he was at the land office of the Canada Company he asked where there was land that no one else wanted. He figured he wouldn't get neighbors that way. He'd rather live alone in a swamp than be with people. But with the discovery of oil, people soon caught up with him. By that time he was ready to come back to the world of the living. It took something more to bring him back to the world of doctoring.

But, there I go, getting ahead of myself again, because I haven't told you about what happened at the house we stopped in for the night. Well, Lemuel figured if I knocked on the door and a lady answered, she wouldn't be scared, so he sent me up to the rough wooden door. It was opened almost as soon as my knuckles hit the wood. But it weren't no lady who answered. It was a boy about my age who smiled at me right off. It wasn't exactly a friendly smile; it was more like a baring of teeth.

Lemuel spoke up because the cat had got my tongue. There I go sounding like Aunt Sadie. I never realized she is so much inside me that I can't get rid of her. It seems I can't run far enough. I hope that's some consolation to her.

"Is there a place we can stay for the night?" Lemuel's voice was gentle and kind. "The barn would be good enough for the likes of us."

"It seems the other gentleman that came didn't think so. He's making himself right at home warming his feet by the fire." The boy pulled a face. "I figure I'll probably have to give up my bed seeing I'm the youngest here."

Now I understood why the smile wasn't real. He probably figured we were shady characters like John, without a care or thought for anyone else, excepting ourselves.

I smiled at him to show I meant no harm to him or his kin. "He's traveling with us, but we don't really know him," I whispered.

"Who is it, Thomas?" A woman's voice came from the warmth of the house.

"Two people, Ma, and they need a place to spend the night."

She came up behind Thomas to look at us. "Well, come in and rest a spell." She opened the door wider and shooed Thomas out of the way so we could enter.

"It's a wretched night to be out." She showed us the hooks on the wall so we could hang up our wet coats.

I was shivering by now and couldn't keep my teeth from chattering. My glasses were fogged up, and my nose running. I wiped it on the back of my sleeve.

"Get the boy some of your clothes, Thomas, or he'll come down with pneumonia, sure enough."

I didn't dare get farther into the house, in case I dragged in more water and mud on that lady's clean floor. Sure it was a board floor, but it was clean. The place was small and cheerful. John was sitting down with another man, talking. Thomas's father got up to introduce himself to us.

"I'm Garrett Johnson, and this here is the missus," he gestured to his wife and to us to sit down on the two wooden chairs by the table.

"Do you have something hot to drink for these travelers, Ma?" His wife went to the sideboard to get a pot of tea that was already steeping.

"Mr. Johnson, I have some horses that need bedding down for the night," Lemuel began in an apologetic voice. "Do you think you have room to spare in your barn?"

"Sure son. I'll get my eldest, Joseph, to do that for you."

At first I hadn't noticed the person sitting on the floor by the stove. He turned a page of the book he was reading by candle light, but he got up quickly when his father said that. I don't suppose he was much older than sixteen. He laid the book gently on the table and went to get a coat. Not a word was said between the two, but the son did as his father said.

I slowly made my way to the side of the table because I wanted to see what he was reading. The title of the book was *Uncle Tom's Cabin*. I had heard of it, but had never read it. It looked like a book I would really like.

Thomas came down the stairs with some dry clothes for me. Lem and John had to do with what they had on. I don't suppose there was any fear of them coming down with pneumonia. People always think I look sickly and try to take care of me. It's enough to make me sick for real.

I went to the corner where Joseph had been and changed there. Mrs. Johnson took my clothes and draped them around the room so they would dry. It was awkward, changing in the same room, but no one seemed to notice. They were all too busy talking about the oil wells to the southwest of us.

Lemuel didn't say much but he was listening, his elbows on his knees and his head cupped in his large hands. He was sitting close to the fire so he could dry out faster. Every now and then you could hear the drip of water on the floor. But he didn't seem to notice or care. Mr. Johnson was talkative enough and shared with them any news he had of the oil town.

He told us it was a rough town full of men and maybe not the best place for a boy like me. Lemuel raised his eyes to look at me when Mr. Johnson said that. I suppose he was regretting taking me. But he never said a word, just listened.

I wish I could have said the same for John. That man could talk the hind leg off of a dog, to use another of my Aunt Sadie's sayings.

John spoke again about California and the gold rush of '49. To hear him tell it you would think he discovered the gold all by himself. He had carriages, a mansion, and a wife. Well, it appeared to me that he probably had none of these things. He either never had them, or he lost them to some foolishness.

"I lost it all in a poker game," he said, as if he could read my thoughts.

That seemed pretty stupid to me, and I almost said so, but Lemuel warned me off with a look. Thomas was sitting next to me and whispered that he wished he could have traveled with Mr. Longville.

"You're welcome to him," I whispered back. "He's a mean old cuss and that's a fact. He left us out in the rain, and we'd be there still, if we didn't have enough sense to follow your light." I pointed to the candle in the window.

Thomas only nodded as if he weren't listening to me. He didn't want to miss a word of what they were saying. John's face looked eerie in the flickering firelight. It cast shadows over his face, making his eyes seem to swivel back in his head and his cheekbones jut out so his head was like a skull. His face was like a warning – like the bell from the fire hall in town, ringing out danger.

Joseph read quietly all the while, and I wished I had the courage to talk to him. He was in his own world and wanted it that way. Books were like that for me too, and I didn't feel I could bother him.

I must have dozed off because I felt Lemuel shaking me and getting me up to go to the barn. John claimed he had weak lungs, so he needed to sleep indoors. They put him on a blanket in front of the fire.

Lemuel and I headed outdoors. The stars were out. The rain had stopped. It was a clear night. Things would be more hopeful in the morning. Mrs. Johnson had given us a crazy quilt and a woollen blanket to take with us. Lemuel checked on the horses while he ordered me to the loft. Because he was holding the lantern, I couldn't see so well where I was going once I climbed the ladder. I crawled carefully around looking for a warm pile of straw. I flattened it out somewhat to make a bed for the two of us. It would be warmer if we slept close together.

The rustle of the straw, the smell of the hay (I knew better than to sleep on the valuable hay) made me realize how fortunate we were to find a place to stay for the night. The Johnsons had been more than amiable. I was wearing borrowed clothes that were clean and neatly patched. I was healthy and lucky to be with my brother. I breathed a sigh of relief and lay down. It wasn't long before Lemuel got down beside me and sheltered me in the crook of his arm.

He fell asleep quickly, his breath fanning my cheek. I stayed awake for a long time wondering what tomorrow would bring. I realized I had come a long way from the boy I was yesterday. I felt sorry for Aunt Sadie now and cried a little before I, too, fell asleep.

I don't know what woke me because it was still mostly dark. I got up and looked out the window of the loft. I saw a man walking from the barn to the house. He looked like John to me.

I didn't think much of it until I smelled smoke. I prodded Lemuel until he rolled over and said grumpily, "What's wrong?"

The smoke drifted up to where we were sleeping, and Lemuel smelled it too. He jumped up and went down the ladder as fast as anything I'd ever seen. I was right behind him.

He found a cigar butt smoldering on a pile of damp straw where there had been a leak in the roof. He stomped on it until it was out.

"Who put that there?" He pointed at the leftover bit of cigar. "You starting smoking now too?"

"It's not me Lem. Honest. I saw John just a minute ago heading back to the house. I don't trust him at all. He looks at me mean-like all the time and then turns and smiles at you. I think he's sort of like a snake, a big one hiding in the grass, waiting for someone to come along and step on him. Then he'll strike and –" My hands were moving with my story and I was just getting into it when Lem hauled me up short.

"That's enough, before your imagination runs away with you. He came out to have a cigar and accidentally threw it on this here pile. He probably aimed for the doorway and missed."

Well, it looked to me like the door was a fair piece from the pile, but what did I know? If I kept on talking Lem would start whistling or something to let me know he wasn't listening. He was giving John the benefit of a doubt, but I wasn't.

"Mark my words, he's a snake in the grass."

It was as if Aunt Sadie was standing right next to me and telling it plain. It felt like she was warning me against this man.

I suddenly missed her even though I was headed for Oil Springs and I was planning on staying there. I would make myself so useful to Uncle Amos that he would let me stay with him forever and ever, amen.

CHAPTER

4

Lemuel looked at the pink horizon and the pearly gray of the sky that meant morning was here for sure. I looked too. Silent. Early morning is beautiful and makes you want to be quiet.

He reached down to muss my hair a bit and then he smiled. "Might as well hitch up the horses and pay the Johnsons for the food, and we'll get an early start."

"Should I go wake John?" I asked.

"Well, we brought him. I don't think the Johnsons want a permanent guest. Titus, remember not to say anything to the Johnsons about the cigar. Mr. Longville is just a bit careless. We'll just take him away from here and no one will be the wiser."

I must have looked concerned and worried because he bent down a bit to get closer to my height. "We're responsible for him now. But, when we get to Oil Springs he can fend for himself. I don't imagine Uncle Amos would take too kindly to having another surprise house guest since he already has one."

I hung my head. "I'll make it up to you both and really help with all the work. I'm not very big, but I'm strong."

As if to prove my words I grabbed one of the collars off of the wall and started to put it on the horse. I stumbled under its weight. The pole straps and traces were hanging next to the other collar. Lemuel watched me some before he came to help. Between the two of us we were done in short order. The sky was totally light by now, and Mr. Johnson came out of the house as we came out of the barn.

"Up and about I see," he said, as if he approved of us.

He pulled Lemuel aside and walked along to the other side of the barn to have a private word. I knew enough not to follow. The murmur of voices was all I could hear. When they came back, Mr. Johnson smiled and told me to get up to the house, and the missus would fix me something to eat. In the meantime he and Lemuel would take the horses on back to the road and try get the wagon unstuck. Mr. Johnson brought his own team to help.

Back at the house John was eating breakfast, and I joined him. When we finished, we thanked Mrs. Johnson and left to meet Lem.

John lit up a cigar. I watched him and said, "You should be more careful with those. You could've burned the barn down this morning."

It was all so fast I didn't realize what was happening. John had me up against the fence with his hands around my neck. He was almost lifting me from the ground.

"You breathe a word, kid, and you'll be sorry. You got to respect your elders. Don't put your nose where it's not wanted."

John made a move as if to burn me with the cigar that was still in his mouth. He then let go and puffed some smoke in my face.

I don't know why I didn't keep quiet, but I didn't. "You talk big when Lem's not around, but you're just a mean, big, fat liar. If you think I believe half of —"

I never got to finish the sentence because he had his hands around my neck again. This time it was John who wasn't so lucky. Lem grabbed his arms and yanked him away from me. I slumped on the ground, breathless. Lem hauled off and punched him good. I heard a loud thunk and saw John lying on the ground, alongside me. He was out like a light. I guess I forgot to mention that

Lem is as strong as an ox and once he's riled, well sir, you have to watch out.

I got up slowly. "We should just leave him here."

Lem was still angry and turned on me, "Leave him for the Johnsons? You think that's a way to repay their hospitality?"

I put my hands in the air and backed up. "Just a suggestion. Does that mean we're stuck with him? Ask him for the twenty dollars before we take him any farther."

"Can't you ever shut up?" Lem asked between his clenched teeth. He was rubbing his sore knuckles. "Just shut up for once."

We didn't have long to wait for John to wake up and rub his jaw. "Dang it all, that hurt, Lem. Doesn't seem right friendly to be hitting me."

"I suppose you thought it was right friendly to be choking me?" I asked.

Lem growled, "Didn't I just tell you to shut up? Now go to the wagon."

I listened that time, even though I don't like injustice and usually try to speak out against it. But even I could see that Lem's patience was at an end.

I don't know what kind of deal Lem made with John, but only minutes later we were all on the wagon heading south once again. I was made to sit in the back. I was happy to be there this time. I could still feel those hands around my neck.

We were lucky that day. The temperature dropped steadily and the going was fine. John sat quietly for the first hour or so, but once the sun warmed him up, his tongue warmed up too. After a while, Lem silenced him with a look.

Lemuel's mouth was in a grim line and he smiled less and less as the day went on. The sun stayed shining even though the temperature plummeted. It was uncomfortable, considering our coats were still damp from the day before.

Occasionally we would come upon other travellers. Sometimes they were in a wagon, other times they were solitary riders. We passed a farmhouse where I could see children finishing up the harvest in the garden. They were digging up turnips and carrots. A little child wandered off from the older ones. The biggest girl rushed after him, her skirt billowing around her. She caught him before he got to the roadway.

I could tell both Lemuel and John found her pretty because they both took off their hats and nodded to her. John yelled out some howdy-do, but Lemuel just smiled and turned to look after her for some time. The girl looked at Lemuel and smiled back. I could see that didn't make a good impression on John for he turned to glare at me.

"What's wrong with you?" I was belligerent. "Girls don't like you none?"

He cuffed me on the head for my pains. Lemuel told me to mind my mouth. I put my arms around my head to protect myself. John sat there smug until Lem told him he would leave him behind if he didn't keep his hands to himself.

I hid my head for a while because I didn't want them to see my tears. They were tears of anger just as much as anything else. I was going to get even with John at some point. I didn't know how or when, but I knew as sure as I knew my name was Titus that I was going to pay him back for the way he treated me.

I was starting to regret leaving London. Everything was a dismal muddy, gray-brown, except for the last remaining leaves on the trees. The reds, browns and yellows could still cheer me, though I was nursing a sore grievance in my breast.

Sitting in a wagon all day can get powerful tiresome, and I asked often enough if we were near Oil Springs yet. I guess I must have asked one time too often because Lemuel turned to me and said, "If you ask that one more time, you're getting out and walking."

It was very quiet that day as the scenery passed us by. Hardly anyone said a word. John would rub his jaw and glance over at Lem with a look of hatred. It would be a long time before he would forget the power of Lem's fist.

The horses had been trotting all day and were thirsty. At a creek up ahead we stopped to water them. The embankment was too steep for the horses and wagon, so I took the two buckets and walked down. The creek was so narrow you could almost stretch your arm across it.

I was daydreaming there, when I heard the sound of a wagon across the river. I looked up to see someone who had the same idea as we did. The land was flat on that side of the creek.

"Hey," I said across the water to the man. The woman stayed on the wagon while he led his horse down.

"Hello son," the man replied. The woman only smiled and pulled her shawl more tightly around her shoulders. She was pale and tired looking. There was a discontented air about her.

"Where you headed Mister?"

"To London."

"That's where we come from." I answered proudly. "My aunt and uncle live there."

"Far from home, I see."

"Yes. I'm with my big brother." I pointed to where Lem and John were standing.

"What you gonna do in London? Visit family?"

"Something like that," the man's answer was non-committal.

Lem was beside me. "My brother is entirely too curious for his own good. You'll have to excuse him."

"No trouble at all," replied the lady. Her voice was whisper thin and hardly carried over the river.

"Where have you come from?" Nothing was going to stop me from asking questions. I had been expected to do the near impossible for the last few days by not speaking. I was tired of being upstaged by John.

"Oil Springs," the man replied. "I'm taking my wife to London and will return back there in a week or two."

"That's where we're headed," there was excitement in Lem's voice. "What's it like? I'm so anxious to get there."

"Well . . ." the man seemed hesitant to say. His wife stayed silent as the grave.

"Is there work there?" Lem didn't seem to notice the man was reluctant to talk.

"Sure there's work for those who aren't lazy. But there's also a lot of men willing to work."

"Is it true that people are getting rich as kings?"

That was my question. There was something about being so rich that interested me. I would like to have a lot of money to spend since I hardly ever got any. Having my own horse and carriage, now that's something I could dream about. I could drive real fast through the streets of London. I thought a bright yellow carriage with red wheels would be beautiful. Heads would turn as I drove past.

"Son, there are no kings in Oil Springs," the woman spoke again and I almost didn't hear her.

"I don't suppose I thought there were." I was defensive. I didn't want her to think I was so silly as to believe there were real kings there. Some people didn't listen real well when a question was asked.

She smiled faintly and turned away. There was bitterness in her eyes, as if someone had hurt her bad.

Her husband answered for her. "It's no place for a lady, or children for that matter. It's kind of rough and tumble," he apologized.

"Sir could I have your name in case I meet you again in town?" Lem asked.

"McCabe, Adam McCabe," he replied.

"I'm Lemuel Sullivan. I'm pleased to make your acquaintance. Ma'am," Lem tipped his hat toward her.

"Now you don't say. You related to Amos Sullivan?"

"Why, yes sir. He's our uncle," I answered for both Lem and me.

"Say hello to him for me and tell him I'll be back as soon as I can."

"Yes sir."

They left and we brought the pails of water up to the horses. Lem took over the job of giving the water to them.

"Probably trying to get to Warwick before nightfall," he said. "His wife looked poorly too. I wouldn't be surprised to find that she's sick."

"Do you suppose there's lots of sickness there, like the fevers?" I was still troubled by my parents' death.

"Even if there is, there's no way to avoid it," Lem said unsympathetically. "It is so much a part of life. If you eat well and work outdoors, I dare say you will stay well and fit as a fiddle."

"I daresay," I murmured.

The horses slurped the water in big gulps. I stood beside them while they drank. My hands were cold and red so I put them under my armpits to warm them up. My breath came in streams of mist. Steam came from the nostrils of the horses too, when they took time to breathe between each drink.

I patted one of them on the face. The one we ended up calling Lady. She was beautiful with gentle brown eyes. She liked my touch, but the one we called Luck wasn't as friendly. I wondered if one day I would be able to ride them or even try handling the wagon. There was so much to wait for while I was growing up, but I'd show them all what I was made of, Aunt Sadie included.

Early on, I had hoped to sit at the front of the wagon for it was tiresome seeing the world backwards. It's nicer to see things as they come to you and not as they pass you by. I didn't dare say anything; afraid Lem would think I was complaining.

To my surprise, Lem invited me to sit between the two men up front. "You won't mind, will you John?"

"No thanks, Lem," I told him. There was no way I was sitting beside John.

"Suit yourself."

John had stopped talking and the silence was worse than hearing him yap on and on. We kept up a steady pace when John mentioned there was smoke in the distance. Someone had a little campfire going. I thought it would be a good idea to go down there and warm up some. We could also eat the last of the food we had packed.

"Could we Lem? I'm pretty near famished," I whee-dled him.

Lem looked at me, then at John. He made his decision. "I don't see why not," he said. "But when I say it's time to leave, don't you argue none." He was looking at me when he said that.

"I won't," I promised.

The horses turned right and followed a cow path. It was a miry mess, but Lem figured we could get through. Well he figured wrong. The wagon was stuck once again. The scent of food rose up to tempt us. It seemed I was always hungry.

"That boy has a hollow leg sure enough," Uncle Robert would say to Aunt Sadie.

"Especially for one so tiny," Aunt Sadie would eye me critically and then decide I needed some medicine. This usually meant giving me castor oil or some other awful-tasting stuff she got at the local apothecary.

We got off the wagon and entered the campsite where there were five men sitting around the fire just swapping stories. Lem stayed behind just long enough to unhitch the horses. Seemed these fellows were headed to Oil Springs too. We sat there awhile feeling good about the warmth. Some men suggested playing a game of cards, and John agreed to it. Lem and I weren't the gambling sort so we declined.

While they were playing, Lem sat down next to me and whispered. "Do you want to keep going?"

"And leave John here?"

Lem nodded grimly.

"What about the wagon?" I was glad that Lem was starting to see reason. We weren't far from Oil Springs anyway, so John could walk it if he had too.

"I'll come back for it tomorrow with Uncle Amos."

We quietly got up and walked toward the bush as if we had private business there. We followed the edge of it until we got to our horses. Lem jumped onto Lady's back and pulled me up behind him. He already had Luck's lead in his hand.

"Giddyap," Lem said.

"Where you guys going?" John hollered at us.

"Go, Lem, go!" I urged.

And off we went flying on the back of Lady with Luck running alongside. The sound of the hooves pounding the earth was like music to my ears. We were heading to Oil Springs without John Longville, trouble-maker and liar. The wagon could wait until tomorrow.

CHAPTER

5

Lem's back was rigid with anger as we rode farther south. He rode the horse hard and I held onto his back, hoping I wouldn't fall off. The wind was cold on my face and my hands. It felt like they were frozen around Lem's middle. I prayed that I wouldn't fall off. My heart was pounding with excitement and I wondered if any of the men would follow us. But, I suppose they knew where we were headed, and they did have our wagon and belongings. The worst part was they had my book and Lem's fiddle.

The wind picked up. There was roaring all around us. It was so loud and so great it started to make me nervous. I tapped Lemuel on the shoulder to get his attention.

"Lem, what's that sound? It's as if something powerful is chasing us."

"What do you mean?"

"The sound of waves rushing in."

"That's no waves."

"What is it then?"

"The wind in the trees."

"It makes me scared."

The roar totally surrounded us, and there was no escaping it. The darkness made the forest seem angry, angry with us for trespassing. It was as if the trees were chasing us to Oil Springs.

We made good time, but it was dark when we entered the village. I saw tall ornamental lamps lighting the main street. Lem told me they used the fuel they distilled from the oil to light these lamps. The place reeked of sulphur. The main street was lined with rooming houses, hotels, and groggeries. People were walking up and down the boardwalk. I saw a horse-drawn bus, just like in London. It was exciting to finally reach our destination. Lem drew the horses up in front of one of the hotels. There were a few men smoking and talking there.

Lem got off Lady, but told me to stay put.

"Lem did he pay you?" I whispered, bending down closer to my brother. I never did see the twenty dollars John owed Lem.

"Hush now, Titus," Lem said. "I'm going to ask directions to Uncle Amos's place. You wait here."

He handed me the reins of the other horse. I could feel Lady's heaving chest beneath me. I was a bit worried that one of the horses would bolt, and I would end up on the ground.

I watched the flickering lamps that lit up the faces of the men as they talked. Lem soon returned. He took over Luck's reins and vaulted onto the horse's back. I was now riding alone, something I had never done before.

"Follow me, Titus," he said as he made his way through the busy street.

After that wild ride through the night I was glad to be almost there – wherever there was. I guided Lady, trying to avoid other carts and horses. It was muddy, and I could hear her hooves squelching beneath me.

Lem stopped in front of a wooden shanty that seemed rooted in the earth. It wasn't very big, but it looked sturdy from what I could see. It was in the village and not outside of it like I pictured it. We would be able to see all the goings on from this house. I was glad of that.

A man came to the doorway when we rode up. You could see the glow of the fire and a lamp behind him. But you couldn't see his face. He was just a big, dark silhouette in the doorway. Uncle Amos was big like Lem. I became worried. He wasn't expecting me.

"Well, Lem, I see you made it, but who's that with

you?" Uncle Amos said. His voice was gentle and my heart took hope.

"It's Titus," Lem replied.

"Titus? The young one?"

"Yes, Uncle Amos."

I didn't have the courage to answer the questions for myself.

"What's he doing so far from home?"

"It's a long story, Uncle Amos. Do you think we could bed the horses down and then come in?"

"Sure, Lem. Wait, while I get the lantern."

Uncle Amos went back in the house. He closed the door behind him. A few seconds passed and he returned with the lantern. He was wearing a warm coat now. We followed him to the small barn behind his house. A larger building loomed beside it. Lem and I began taking the leads off of the horses. A pure white cat climbed the stall walls and walked around, watching us with yellow eyes. I reached out to pet it, but it jumped down quickly and disappeared out of the door.

I still hadn't said a word to my uncle, but did sneak a peek at him now and again while we were in the barn. He had dark hair, like the rest of my family. His beard was big and bushy. His eyebrows came downward in a scowl to his eyes. He looked like my dad, except for the beard. I wasn't sure what to think of him until he caught me looking at him.

He smiled, his teeth showing real white against his black beard. He ruffled my hair as he walked by me to hang up the traces. I ducked my head, embarrassed. Everybody treats me like a little child.

"So Titus, you think you'll like it here?"

Just like that, my uncle accepted my being there. He expected me to stay. There were no words of sending me back or anything like that. He must have figured that if Lem brought me, there must be a good reason for it. He didn't know.

We left the barn, single file. Uncle Amos was in the lead holding the lantern high so we could all see where we were going. I noticed the bits left over in a garden. The cabbage and turnip ends were still there. I figured they would need to be harvested soon.

The door creaked as Uncle Amos opened it, and we all entered. Lem, thankful for the warmth, sat very close to the fire and so did I, though I was on the floor. I took off my damp shoes and socks and put them near the hearth to dry. Uncle Amos put on a kettle of water. He opened a box of dried leaves and put them into a pot. Once he was done with that, he sat with us to wait for the water to boil.

"So let's have the story, shall we?" Uncle Amos put his elbows on his knees and leaned toward the fire. "I suppose you'll have to tell it Lem, seeing as Titus here, is mute."

Lem smiled at that. "You have the wrong of it, Uncle. Titus is rarely quiet."

"He can talk?" Uncle Amos threw up his hands in mock surprise. He was teasing, and I could tell. I knew I was going to like him.

"Of course I can, Uncle Amos." I finally found the courage to speak.

"Still, I think I should tell the story," Lem interrupted. "Seeing as I'm the oldest."

"Can I tell my side of it?"

"Sure you can, once Lem is finished." Uncle Amos got up and poured the hot water into the pot.

The steam rose up in a swirl. I looked at their faces in the lamplight. There was a warm glow to this house, even though it was tiny. The floor was rough wood, but a homemade rug was on the floor under our feet. I curled my toes onto the warmth of it.

Lem told the story of his leaving and my running away without any fancy things to add. He didn't say anything about John, and I was surprised. I guess he figured the less said about John, the better.

When he was done, Uncle Amos leaned back in his chair. He stretched his arms over his head and I could hear the bones cracking in his fingers as he stretched them too. I waited without speaking.

"Now it's your turn, Titus."

"I think Lem said it all," I began cautiously. I wasn't sure if Uncle Amos liked stories so much as the truth.

"Surely he doesn't know the whole story."

"Whatever do you mean Uncle?"

"Does he know why you left?"

"I suppose he does, though I never had the opportunity to tell him."

"Two days on the road and no opportunity?"

"Well, you see, I was a stowaway. But we took in a traveler. His name's John Longville, but we left him behind somewheres north of here. This man could talk the hind leg off'n a dog. So, I never had much chance of talking to Lem."

"A traveling companion, eh?" Uncle Amos laughed and looked to Lem to clear up the story.

"He offered to pay us so I took him, thinking the money would come in handy."

"And he never paid nothin'." My voice was filled with disgust.

"That so?" Uncle Amos looked to Lem.

"He paid half, that was the deal . . . but we left him before he could pay the rest."

You see, sir, I didn't know John paid half. That must've happened after Lem laid him flat don't you think? But we were tired, and Uncle Amos said the rest of the story could be told another day.

"'Pears to me that you two need something to eat and then off to bed."

Uncle Amos cut some bread for us and some hard yellow cheese. It was the best ever, sitting by the fire and toasting that bread on long handled forks that were kept by the hearth. I ate my food quickly and was thankful for it. Uncle Amos piled a few blankets on the floor for us and we slept near the fire.

Sleep came quickly and morning did too. I woke to Uncle Amos whistling. I propped my head on my hand, elbow resting on the floor. I watched him for a while until he noticed me. He pointed his pancake flipper at me.

"Get up you young whipper snapper. I have flapjacks for you."

I nudged Lem. He yawned and blinked a few times until his eyes became accustomed to the light. There were only two small windows in that house, but they gave enough light for us. Aunt Sadie wouldn't have liked it because there were no lace curtains, but I did because there were no lace curtains.

Once we were all at the table eating, Uncle Amos began asking more questions. He wondered if Lem had sent word to Aunt Sadie to let her know where I was. Lem told him that he had written a letter at the first halfway house we came to where we had eaten lunch. Uncle Amos supposed she must have the letter by now.

"I don't suppose you thought about her worrying, did you?" He looked at me serious-like.

"No sir, I didn't, at least not until we had gone a far piece from home."

I guess that's not the whole truth because I did think about worrying her, but it didn't bother me none. I figured she deserved it, but I wasn't going to say anything about that to Uncle Amos because I wanted him to think good of me.

Uncle Amos seemed lost in thought. Then he spoke again. "I want you to write a letter today and tell her how sorry you are that you worried her. I want to read the letter before you send it off."

After breakfast he gave me a paper and pencil and I sat at the table composing the letter to Aunt Sadie. At first I didn't know where to begin and said as much. "At the beginning," was Uncle Amos's answer as he cleaned the dishes.

After checking it, Uncle Amos added some words to it, but I didn't read them. He folded the paper and put some sealing wax on it. He told me where the post office was and gave me money for a stamp. I wondered what he had written, but whatever it was, it helped me to stay with him because it wasn't until Christmas that I saw Aunt Sadie again.

As soon as I was out the door I ran to the main street. I looked back at Uncle Amos's place and saw that a new house was being built behind the shanty. There were wooden buildings all around me. It was a crowded town, and walking down the side streets felt like I was in a maze. I passed mostly men on my way but I saw a couple of children too.

You could post letters from George Yates's store. I found it easy because there was a sign on the outside that read POST OFFICE. Men stood at the front of the office around a spittoon talking. Though I longed to stand and listen, I knew it was rude so I walked into the store with my eyes to the ground. One man pulled the brim of my hat down as I walked past.

"You the young-un staying with Amos Sullivan?"

I scuffed the toe of my boot along the boardwalk. "Yes, sir."

News sure traveled fast in that town.

"Figure you can work in the oil fields boy?" Another man asked.

"I don't rightly know, seeing as I never done so before."

"Can you drive a team of horses?"

I looked up to see the man smiling and realized he was teasing me. I clutched the letter in my hand, wrinkling it. "No, sir. Horses are big creatures and I suppose they need someone stronger than me to look after them."

"You figured that right, boy."

He smiled again. In fact all the men smiled, then one pointed to my letter and he gave me a nickel.

"Go in and get yourself a treat while mailing that letter."

That man was James Wakefield, though I didn't know it at the time. He was a very good friend of my Uncle Amos. I wasn't used to people handing me money for candy, so I stood awkwardly for a second or two then I blurted out. "Thank you. Much obliged."

The men all laughed. I guess my politeness amused them. They were used to rougher ways, living out here on the oil frontier. I could feel my blush and wished I wasn't quite so embarrassed.

Once I entered I tried to straighten out the letter by flattening it against the counter in the store. I pressed my palms down on it, leaving a few dirty streaks. I sighed realizing it was almost impossible to keep anything clean out here. Even the counter was dingy with dirt.

I went up to Mr. Yates and paid for a stamp. Then I took a little longer trying to decide what to buy with the nickel. He had a jar full of peppermint sticks so I got one for me and one for Lem. I headed back to Uncle Amos's house thinking he would have some work for me to do once I got there.

Well, sir, I don't know if you remember the first time you saw a Negro, but I can remember it as clear as day. I was walking along enjoying the sights. A window opened above me and a girl leaned out with a cloth that she shook out vigorously. I was looking up at her when she smiled at me. I tipped my hat to her, which made her laugh. I put the hat back on my head and turned quickly, only to bump into someone.

He was a boy my age. His face was a dark color like the beautiful walnut sideboard Aunt Sadie had in the dining room. His eyes were shining and he seemed friendly because he had a wide smile on his face. I smiled right back. We became friends just like that. All it took was two smiles. I held out my hand to shake, saying, "I'm Titus Sullivan."

"Moses Croucher." He shook my hand.

I took the other peppermint stick out of my shirt pocket and handed it to him. I brushed off the little bit of lint on it first. "Some man gave me a nickel to get a treat. I bought two, so this one's for you."

Moses's eyes lit up, and he took the stick breaking it in two. "I'm gonna give this piece to Beulah, my sister."

I thought of the loaves and the fishes, how Jesus made them multiply. I broke the end off of my stick and put it in my pocket for Lem. What had begun as a treat for one became a treat for four.

"Where you headed?" Moses asked me.

"To my uncle's home."

"We could hitch a ride here and drive to the end of the way and ride back again." Moses pointed at the horse-drawn buses that went up and down the main street many times in the day. They brought the oilmen to and from the fields. It saved them lots of time. I pulled out the three pennies left in my pocket.

"Will this be enough?"

"Sure." Moses ran ahead of me to catch the bus that was leaving from in front of the Oxford House.

I jumped up behind him as the driver warned Moses. "Here, boy, you ain't paid your fare."

Moses glared at him and I put the pennies in the man's hand. "Will that be enough for the two of us?"

"Just this once. Next time be prepared to pay more."

"How much more, sir?"

The man never answered me, and the wagon jolted so that I sat down more quickly than I planned. Moses and I laughed at that though I felt I had the stuffing knocked out of me a bit.

"Why was he like that?" I asked Moses.

Moses shrugged his shoulders, but I could see he was hurt and angry at the same time. The man had talked differently to me than to Moses. I was sure of that. I thought it might be because of the color of his skin. I sat thinking there for a while, and Moses asked me why I was so quiet.

I shrugged my shoulders back at him. I wasn't a little kid anymore, and I knew Moses's pa must have been a slave before he came to Canada. We all knew that's why the war was going on to the south of us. When we got off at the end of the main street we were quiet, our high spirits deflated.

"That wasn't as much fun as I planned on," Moses said.

"It weren't any fault of yours," I said trying to be cheerful. "Sometimes adults are the most hard-brained people in the world. Don't figure you should let it bother you none. He's just one man."

"If only he was just one man," Moses replied thoughtfully.

"What do you mean?" I was puzzled. I didn't seem to understand that the man could be more than one man. But that isn't what Moses meant, and I know that now.

We stood on the sidewalk trying to come up with something to do when we heard shouts coming from the east of us. I looked to where people were pointing and saw billows of black smoke rising into the air. The cry of "Fire" ripped through the air around us.

CHAPTER

6

The smoke was coming from the creek. Moses led the way, since he knew the area better than me. I followed him, trying to keep up with his long legs. He ran very fast. People kept jostling me and getting in the way. I lost sight of him a few times. Once I was almost knocked down, but some man held on to me so I wouldn't fall. He pulled me aside and let the flow of people by.

"Don't suppose Amos would thank me much if I let you get trampled underfoot. Follow me."

I looked up to see James Wakefield. The man knew a shortcut and we headed down to the creek. It was an awesome sight seeing the creek on fire.

"What makes it do that?" Everyone knows that water doesn't burn.

"There's oil slicks on the top of the water. Some-one's still must've been too close to the creek. Not the first time it's happened."

"How . . . can . . . it . . . be . . . stopped?" I had been running and was out of breath and my words came out slowly and painfully. I hunched over and put my hands on my knees. Mr. Wakefield had disappeared into the thick smoke.

It was an inferno. Flames leaped and danced in a frenzy. The smoke billowed straight up and then drifted over the town. People were coughing and trying to see clear of the smoke. I didn't want to get too close to the creek. Not only was the heat unbearable, I knew I would only be in the way. My eyes were hurting and my glasses were completely dirty. I tried to wipe them clean on my shirt, but that just made them a blurry mess, so I put them in my pocket next to the bit of peppermint stick.

I couldn't find Moses. I walked without knowing where I was going. I bumped into people, apologizing as I went. I couldn't get my bearings because nothing was familiar. The voices were loud all around me. Sweat dripped down my forehead, into my eyes. Now I was really blind and afraid. I stood still and wondered what I should do next. Someone bumped into me, and I didn't think anything of it because I had been bumped into a bunch of times already.

I wanted someone to rescue me. Then I had the sense to call out. I yelled out Moses's name. "Stop hollering. He ain't gonna come down from heaven to help you no matter how loud you yell." It was a girl's voice at my elbow.

"I ain't callin' *that* Moses," I tried to put as much anger in my voice as possible.

Though I hated to have help from a girl, I asked for it anyway. "I can't see. Could you help me find a place to sit down, out of the way?"

The girl took me by the hand. Her hand was rough in mine, like she was used to hard work. She led me away from the heat. I kept stumbling over mud clods on the road, made slippery with oil and mud.

"Slow down or I'll fall," I protested.

"You ain't gonna fall. Just hang on."

She jerked my arm and pulled me along. I followed as best as I could. The smoke started clearing up a little and I could make out a building ahead of us. We scrambled up the wooden sidewalk, and she took me to a bench that was in front of a store. She was bent over me.

I wiped my eyes with the back of my shirtsleeve. I could see her now, and she was beautiful. I jerked my head back away from her, because she was getting too close to me and it was uncomfortable. She stepped back in annoyance.

"What's wrong with you? I wasn't gonna bite."

Whenever I was around girls I got awkward and stumbled over my words. That happened this time too, so I stopped talking except to say, "Thank you for your help. I can look after myself now."

"I suppose you kin see now!" She had her hands on her hips and looked at me sternly. "How'd you git your eyesight back? Moses help you?"

I laughed, pulled my glasses out of my pocket and tried to clean them with my shirttail. The girl grabbed them out of my hand and went to the horse trough for water. She dipped the glasses in and then proceeded to clean them on her apron. When she thought they were clean enough, she handed them back to me. I put them on my nose and gazed at her. Seeing clear didn't change her appearance one bit. She still looked good to me. Then she put a cloth in the water to wet it and wrung it out a little. I wasn't sure what she was going to do with that.

The flames and smoke were still there, but we weren't in the thick of it. I wondered what happened to Moses and if I could find him before I headed home. While I was sitting there thinking, the girl was tapping her foot with impatience. She stared down at me and was about to say something when it seemed like she changed her mind. She did this a couple of times and then finally took a deep swallow.

"You should be fine now. I'm going down there to have a look-see." Her voice had the music of the Irish tongue.

I got up from where I was sitting. "I'm coming along."

"No, you're not. You're a wee mon that needs caring for."

"I'm not wee," I was indignant. "I'm almost as old as you."

"Don't give yourself airs." She looked daggers at me. "I'm fourteen, and that's a fact."

Though my birthday wasn't for another ten months, I told her I was thirteen. You could see she didn't believe me by the look on her face. But to tell you the truth, she lied to me too. She was only thirteen herself, not much more than a year older than me.

"Well, almost," I admitted sullenly. "My birthday will be here soon enough."

"When?"

"Soon enough."

She turned away with a huff and jumped down into the muddy, oily mess that was the street. Some splashed back on her skirt, but she didn't notice.

I jumped down behind her. "What's your name?"

"Mercy, Mercy Merriman."

"Titus Sullivan, that's me."

We both walked down toward the creek. The commotion was still all around us and I kept looking for Moses. The smoke was a bit less thick because the fire was headed downstream. There was no chance I was going to be blinded again and at the mercy of a girl named Mercy. She put the wet cloth to her mouth, and I followed her billowing skirt as best I could. If I concentrated on what was just ahead of me I could see well enough where I was going. People were coughing and cursing and trying to put out the fire. It was hard to tell what they were doing because I was too far from the real action. I didn't dare go any closer though. Mercy had left me far behind by now.

I stopped for a minute to catch my breath and wondered how I could have lost both Moses and Mercy all in one day. My lungs were fit to bursting with the black smoke. I thought maybe I had best head back to Uncle Amos's house. I had had enough excitement for one day.

Uncle Amos was at the door to meet me. "I got worried about you, boy. Where've you been?"

"Lost in the smoke. It's so dark." In truth it was like night had fallen over the whole town. I was coughing by this time. Uncle Amos watched me with a very concerned look.

"Best to stay inside. I'm going to go see how I can help. If it spreads down the creek, other communities like Wilkesport will be affected. Can't have that now, can we?" He left without glancing back, disappearing in the thick, black smoke.

I was tired of coughing and went into the house. It was going to be very strange living here. Uncle Amos had prepared a pallet on the floor for the two of us. I lay down and stared at the ceiling that was covered in cobwebs. A spider caught a fly in its web. The drone of the frantic fly gave me the loneliest sensation. After awhile I just fell asleep and didn't wake up until Uncle Amos and Lemuel came into the house.

"That was amazing and scary," Lemuel began. "I didn't think we'd ever get it out. There's some right smart-thinking men in this community."

Uncle Amos lit a lamp and then bent down to the hearth. He moved the coals around a bit and put another piece of wood on the fire. Hours had passed between me coming home and most of the blaze being put out. The air was a little clearer, but I looked out the window and could still see a glow from the flames. The stink of smoke and oil hung heavy in the air.

I leaned up on my elbow. "The fire's not out. I still see it." I said.

"We chopped down trees." Lemuel sat on the pallet beside me. His eyes were bright with the excitement of battling the huge inferno. "Many of us went downstream on horseback."

"Whatever for?"

"They wanted us strong guys to cut trees."

"To cut trees?"

"Yeah. We cut them down and spread them across the creek. Others cut sod and collected clay from the banks. We made a huge dam. There was nowhere for the fire to go after that."

"It'll eventually burn itself out." Uncle Amos said.

I smiled up at my big brother. "I wish I could've helped you. I couldn't see through the smoke and my glasses were all dirty . . ."

"Don't worry none, Titus. Men were needed for this work."

I knew Lem was trying to comfort me, but it only made me feel worse to realize I was so weak and shortsighted.

I looked down at my pale hands and felt shame. They were tiny next to my brother's big work-rough hands. I put them under my legs, trying to hide them.

Uncle Amos turned to me, "You'll be helping like that soon enough. Why, by next summer I wouldn't be surprised if you've grown half a foot."

There must have been doubt in my eyes 'cause when I looked up at him he said, "Honest and truly, you will grow, Titus."

I could feel the heat rise up to my face. Lem looked back and forth at the two of us, mighty puzzled. Lem was big, strong, and true, but he surely wasn't the smartest of the lot. I smiled at them both and kept my thoughts to myself. I had to see it first to believe it.

The thing that puzzled me the most about Uncle Amos was that he was so different from what Aunt Sadie had said about him. She even called him a disgrace. He didn't seem a disgrace to me at all. No sir. He is the most honorable man I ever met.

Lem looked like he was ready to drop off any minute. Uncle Amos was stirring something in a pot over the fire. I went over to help him. He asked me to cut some bread and pour water into cups. As the pot warmed up, the smell of rabbit stew filled the air. Lem was leaning against the wall, his eyes closed, his face black. I imagine mine was too. Uncle Amos had washed his in the basin by the door. Drops of water shone in his beard.

"How long before the air clears?" Lem asked, opening his eyes. He coughed into his hand and looked at Uncle Amos.

"A day or two. That was one huge conflagration. I wouldn't be surprised if Sadie and Robert could see the smoke all the way in London."

Lem's eyes widened. "That'd be amazing. The smell is horrific. I didn't reckon on it when I decided to come out here. It'll take some getting used to, right Titus?"

"It sure will, but I like everything else. Except for the forest."

In fact, the bush that surrounded this town was so thick and swampy it was creepy just to walk out into it. I'd had enough of it when we came here on horseback. But I supposed we would have to go through it again to get Lem's fiddle and wagon back. I didn't dare whine about my book or penny whistle.

CHAPTER

7

Tom Abrams, our neighbor, was a reporter for the new paper called the *Oil Springs Chronicle*. The banner at the top of it read *And the Rock poured me out Rivers of oil.*

It was dusk, Tom was coming down the main street, and the creek was still burning. Everything was blue and gray except for the flare of orange color. Mercy walked behind him, intent on her own thoughts. Lem and Uncle Amos were in the house, trying to rustle up some supper.

Tom sat on the wooden stoop beside me and began talking about the day's events. It had taken hours to build the dam and everyone was exhausted. Mercy plopped down beside Tom as if she had known us all for a long time. Tom smiled and said hello, then looked at me as if asking how I knew her. Mercy exclaimed over the size of the fire.

"That was the largest yet," she said grimly. "Not the first, nor will it be the last, but it was the worst."

"Folks got to be more careful where they place the hot coke," Tom replied.

"Hot coke?" I asked.

"They use it as fuel for the refineries."

"You'd think they'd move the refineries away from the crick." Mercy sniffed and wiped her face with her sleeve.

"Where'd you go?" I asked her.

"Downstream a bit. I watched the men cut the trees and helped get sod and clay to pile on the dam."

I was sorry to have missed the action. Even a girl had done more than me. Tom must have understood how I felt because he turned to me and said kindly, "There'll be other fires, believe me. You'll have hordes of opportunities to be heroic in this town."

Mercy laughed. It was her laughter that lured Lemuel out of the house. As soon as Mercy saw him I knew something was up. She sat straighter and smoothed out her blackened gown. "I saw you cut the trees."

Lem smiled. "Me and a bunch of other guys."

"You related to him?" she asked me, pointing to Lem.

"My brother. Lem, this is Mercy Merriman."

"Miss Merriman," Lem almost bowed over her hand. I'm sure Mercy blushed, though it was hard to tell under all that dirt.

I scooted over to make room for Lem, and he sat between the two of us. We talked quietly as the dark descended. Then we went in, inviting Mercy to eat with us. Tom stayed for supper too, and it was a nice way to end the evening. The glow of the lamps hanging on the wall shone on the circle of friends. I felt real happy. I knew I had done right to come here. Here was where I belonged.

CHAPTER

8

The next few days the wind picked up and the swampy bush became a dark and noisy place. Aunt Sadie would have said it was unnerving. It roared like a huge beast stalking its prey. I covered my ears often.

I stayed in the comfort of the cabin, though Aunt Sadie would have laughed at my notion of comfort. There was little enough in it to appeal to most women. That's why the town had very few women compared to the hordes of men. There was no real comfort there, only adventure and thick, black oil that slurped around our feet if a wildcatter couldn't stem the flow from his well soon enough.

Uncle Amos and Lem went to retrieve the wagon we had left behind, but they came back empty-handed. Lem supposed it was possible he was mistaken about the exact place, but the ruts said otherwise. It was a hard lesson learned: never to leave your belongings behind, even if you're trying to escape someone as wily as John Longville.

Occasionally, Uncle Amos and Lem would make a run to Sarnia with someone's oil on the new plank road. It usually took a couple of days to do a run, so Tom would come and stay with me. Tom lived with his brother, another oilman.

I suppose you're wondering what happened to John Longville and how he came to town. I don't rightly know when he arrived, but one day Tom and I went down to Yates's store for supplies and there he was.

Many of the local oilmen came from the United States of America, and were very interested in what was going on back home. There was a group of them sitting outside listening to someone reading a newspaper that had news from the south. One made a disparaging remark about "darkies," while another laughed.

"Well, there seems to be enough of them here. It's like I'm right back home."

I turned to the speaker because I recognized John Longville's voice.

Tom stared at him too. "You have a problem with that?" he asked.

John grunted and then noticed me. "I shoulda known you'd be hanging around with another troublemaker."

"Are you referring to him or me?" Tom asked, pointing at me as he spoke.

"That kid is nothing but trouble," John announced. "He and his brother walked off with ten dollars of mine."

I was too surprised to answer that unjust accusation. We never even saw the ten dollars, let alone stole it from him.

"Don't say anything," Tom instructed me under his breath. "I sincerely doubt that," he said, as he walked into the store. I followed him, not wanting to be left behind.

"How do you know John?" Tom asked, looking out of the window.

"He traveled with us here."

"He's a friend?"

"No." I shook my head vigorously.

"Well, he's nothing but trouble," Tom said. "He's trying to rile up people about the Negroes working on the wells."

"Why's he doing that?"

"Says they work for less pay, and he thinks they're taking jobs away from the likes of him."

"Do they *want* to work for less pay?"

"I don't imagine." Tom was watching the men closely while he talked. "I'd recommend you steer clear of him. He seems to have it in for you. By the way, what's all this about ten dollars?"

"He promised Lem twenty dollars to bring him here with us, but I think he only paid ten. You best ask Lem."

I puzzled over what Tom had told me and wondered about my friend Moses, who was always working while I was in school. Moses said I was lucky to be learning, but that he needed to help out his family. I didn't see it that way. I would rather have been with the men in the oil fields.

I was supposed to go to school every day, but truth be told I was bored most of the time. With all the excitement going on around me it was hard to concentrate on my reading, writing, and 'rithmetic. I never did tell Uncle Amos I wasn't attending school regular. Sometimes I would just head on out in the morning and come back around the time he was expecting me. And that's what I did all the next week. I watched the men work instead of attending school. I did like my teacher, Mrs. Ryan, but she was not enough to keep me there.

Moses and I would wander off for a bit, if his daddy gave him permission. One day, I went to Adam McCabe's well and stopped to talk to him. That's when I saw Moses, working on one of the wells. It was his turn to operate the kickboard. The tapping sound of it rang through the bush. It was like he was dancing a jig because you had to put your whole body into the work. It looked like something I might like to try, so I went up to Moses and asked him if I could. He smiled at me, but shook his head.

"My turn's almost up," he told me. "Then we'll go down to the creek."

While I waited, I watched the men at their work. Getting oil out of the ground is a mighty interesting task. I was learning about the spring pole that Moses was operating. Usually the pole was a cut-down ash tree. You tied it down at one end. At the opposite end, a really heavy drilling bit was attached by a chain. This chain was put down into the already dug well. Then a type of lever was built over the hole and attached to the ash pole. If you stepped on this lever, or kickboard, the pole would lift, and the drill bit would go deeper into the rock. When the bit worked its way through the rock, someone would add another length of chain so it could drill even farther. When you hit oil, you would have to jump back, or you'd get it all over yourself. The work was hard.

The swamp was full of black ash trees and the men

chopped them down to make derricks. They were like tepees sitting over the wells. The men attached a winch to each tepee so they could haul the tools out of the hole by cranking them up on a cable.

Moses made kicking the springboard look easy, so I asked again if I could try. He got off, and I got on, hardly missing a beat. I tried my best to keep it at the same pace as Moses, but I guess I failed.

"Hey you. What do you think you're doing?" a man yelled. "This is not job for kids. Move along. Moses . . ."

He didn't have to finish his sentence. Moses knew he'd better get back to work. I felt embarrassed. It wasn't my fault I was small for my age. But Moses's daddy came along and told Moses he could take the rest of the day off.

We ran down the nearest path, intending to come back after taking a look at the creek. A little farther along, we came upon a wagon just sitting there in a little clearing. That wagon looked mighty familiar. I went up and looked at it closely. It was definitely my brother's wagon. I was excited and so was Moses when I told him the story. We decided then and there to bring the horses and Lem and get our wagon out of that bush.

As we walked back to town, we got this really good idea. We'd use the wagon for driving people around the oilrigs. Seems people from other towns were really interested in seeing what an oil rush looked like, and often they had to wait for the omnibus to return from its rounds. The more we talked about it, the more we liked the idea. We could even make some money doing it. The only problem would be to convince Uncle Amos and Lem to let us use the team and wagon.

As we entered the main street, we bumped into Mercy. She was heading back to work at her aunt and uncle's hotel. We told her about the wagon and our idea. She was excited for us too.

I mentioned that Lem's fiddle, my penny whistle and book had been left on the wagon when we ran off to Oil Springs. Mercy listened and said she might know exactly where that fiddle and my things could be.

"There's a man called John who asked my aunt to put them in a safe place. I thought they were his things, but I bet they are yours."

This was good news to me. "Do you think you can try and get them back for us? Lem's a good fiddler, and I'll get him to play for you."

"My aunt watches me like a hawk. I'll try, but I'm not promising anything."

This was enough for me. We thought we'd follow her to the hotel and distract her aunt who was named

Mrs. Mabee, while Mercy headed for the back room to get our things. Mrs. Mabee was at the front desk talking to some men when we entered.

"Well there you are, finally," she scolded Mercy. "What took you so long? Rooms 210 and 211 need to be cleaned right away."

Mercy looked at us apologetically. "Maybe later?" she whispered.

Mrs. Mabee noticed Moses standing next to me. "Can I help you?" she asked with a sneer.

"No ma'am," Moses replied politely. "I'm waiting here with Titus."

"Well we don't serve your kind here." Mrs. Mabee's voice was firm.

I got into arguing with her right there and then and nodded at Mercy to go get the things while we diverted her aunt. Mrs. Mabee was loud and cruel the way she talked about Moses, and I kept arguing to give Mercy time.

The men watched. Some were uncomfortable, but the one named Max joined in with Mrs. Mabee.

"You want I should throw him out?" he asked, moving closer to Moses.

I jumped between the two. "Don't you dare touch my friend."

Max pushed me aside like I was a flea, then pulled Moses toward the door. I ran behind them and kicked Max real hard in the leg a couple of times. He turned and pushed me so hard I fell on my backside to the floor. By the time I got up Moses was outside and Max was coming for me. Next thing I knew, I was out on the street next to Moses.

"Well, we created a diversion," I remarked while brushing off the dirt. Mrs. Mabee didn't keep the cleanest hotel.

Moses didn't say anything, he was that angry. He stalked off until I called to him. "Come on, don't let them ruin our day. We'll get even with them somehow."

At the rear of the hotel, Mercy was waiting with our things. "Is this your stuff?" she asked.

"Yes. Thank you. Thank you, Mercy. Lem will be glad to have his fiddle back."

So Moses and I went to Uncle Amos's place and watched the men at work building the new house. It was going to be very large. Lem finally showed up, and we told him about the wagon. He put the traces and harnesses on the horses and let the whiffle tree drag behind. The three of us set off to retrieve the wagon.

Moses and I got to ride while Lem led the horses, talking to them gently as we passed down the main street.

The mud wasn't so bad today because much of the ground was frozen. I was quite excited about getting the wagon back – until we got near enough to see four men standing around it. And there, sure enough, was John Longville sitting on it like he owned the darned thing.

"Heard these boys were snooping around my wagon. Thought I'd come back to protect my property." John spat on the ground.

"You know well enough, John, that there wagon belongs to me," Lem replied.

"Prove it." John spat again. This time the gob landed very near Moses's feet.

"Watch where you're spitting, mister," Moses said.

John let one fly that caught onto Moses's shirtsleeve. Lem was on that wagon quicker than a wink. He pushed John into the back of the wagon and the two of them set to wrestling. I got a handful of frozen grass and tried to wipe the stuff off of Moses's sleeve.

The men seemed to enjoy watching the wrestling match and I have to admit most were betting on Lem winning. He was much bigger than John. It was done soon enough, and Lem dragged a groggy John off the wagon and set him on the ground.

"You asked me to prove it," Lem said and showed John where he had written his name underneath the step board. A couple of the men ducked down to read it too.

"There's his name plain enough, John," said one man pointing at it.

"Well 'pears to me you owe me delivery money. I delivered this here wagon to town for free."

Two of the men walked off disgusted with John's lying. Only two stayed to see what would happen.

"That seems fair enough," one of them said hesitatingly. He didn't want to feel the power of Lem's fists.

"How much?" Lem asked through clenched teeth.

"Twenty dollars."

"Twenty?" Lem roared. "Are you mad?"

John took a step back. "I'll settle for ten. That seems fair doesn't it?" The two bystanders nodded in agreement. They probably figured they could all go down to one of the groggeries and get something to drink with that money.

Lem figured he might as well give the ten dollars because he paid it to John right then and there. John and the two men walked off but not before John yelled out to Moses, "You damn darkies should stay in your place. You got no business here."

CHAPTER

9

"Lem, we got your fiddle back today too," I said as we drove away from the clearing in the woods.

"That's good," Lem said. "I suppose John had that too."

"Yup he did, but Mercy got it back for us."

"Well, tell her thanks," Lem said.

Moses seethed on the drive back, and I was angry too, not knowing what to say to him. I wasn't used to people treating each other badly. Oh, Aunt Sadie would complain about me all the time, but I knew in some small way she still cared for me. John was different. He was cruel for the sake of being cruel.

Well sir, for the use of the wagon Lem wanted a cut of the money we earned taking people around town, but I complained we were the ones who found it in the first place. In the end we agreed that I would give Lem the first five dollars I earned – half of the "delivery money" John had demanded. Uncle Amos didn't know nothing about it though. I asked Lem to keep it a secret so I could surprise Uncle Amos once the business was up and running. But Uncle Amos found out soon enough without a word being breathed by Lem.

The most exciting days were when the people came from big cities like Toronto and Boston, just to look around. They expected prime service from hotels and locals, and they were willing to pay for it. What they didn't reckon on was that most of the men here were able to pay well for services too. The discovery of oil was making men richer than they ever thought they would be.

Outside of the Oxford, Moses and I saw a group of people standing around, wanting to see the oilrigs. The omnibus that runs up and down the main road could only take them so far. This was our chance. We drove our wagon up to them and made them pay ten cents each to get on. We did a few runs that day, before I drove Moses to his house on Crooked Line and then returned home.

The next Saturday we saw a group of people standing in front of the Michigan Exchange Hotel. They definitely looked out of place. The women wore nice clothes, and everyone was clean. No oil had touched the hems of their dresses yet. Moses pulled up next to them and doffed his hat.

We had decided that I should be the spokesman, since I looked young for my age and people were impressed with my way of talking.

"Ladies and gentlemen, we are at your service. If you wish for a pleasant, eventful tour of our illustrious town of Oil Springs, you have only to say the word, and we will see to it that you discover every nook and cranny of the oil industry. You too, will experience the excitement and the fever that has claimed these men's souls."

I stopped for breath and a rich-looking gentleman stepped forward. "How much do you charge for this adventure, young men?" he asked, smiling. I could tell he was amused by my little talk.

"Only twenty-five cents each," I astonished myself at this boldness, when we usually only charged a ten-cent piece.

The gentleman didn't bat an eye. "You can see we have seven of us who wish this pleasure. Here is one dollar and seventy-five cents." He pulled out some money and handed it to me. Moses grinned.

There were three ladies in the bunch, and I got out of the wagon to help them into it. That's when I realized one of the women was my teacher, Mrs. Ryan. Her bonnet had hidden her face from me.

"So here's where you spend your days when you're not at school!" she chided me.

"Yes ma'am," I hung my head down, trying to look sorry, though I wasn't. We had laid an extra plank to serve as a seat so more people could go at the same time. Mercy had made us some cushions so it would be more comfortable. The women sat down gingerly, afraid of soiling their gowns.

Mrs. Ryan wanted to sit at the front but ended up in the back with the rest of them. She was bright-eyed and taking everything in.

"Do your parents know you aren't at school most days?" she asked cheerfully from the back.

"Don't have any parents," I mumbled.

"With whom do you live then?" she asked.

I ignored her and began to answer the questions that were being fired at me by the gentlemen. We stopped at the creek to show them the sheen of oil that always smeared its surface. Moses told them about the fire and how it had been put out. They were fascinated by the fact that fire was a common enough occurrence around here. One woman shuddered and vowed she could never live in such a "backwater place."

We took them to Shaw's gusher where men were working. There was oil on the ground near the well, and the men wore boots to keep their feet dry. The stench was very strong, and the women took out handkerchiefs soaked in cologne to cover their noses.

We told them how Mr. Shaw spent months hoping to strike oil. No one had drilled that deep for oil before, but he kept working at it until one day, as Uncle Amos would tell it "The ground shuddered, a loud crack was heard, and the mouth of the earth opened up and spewed out black, odorous muck."

A lot of people thought Shaw was crazy at the time, but now he's a rich man. I told them that people now spoke of him with reverence. Tom said Mr. Shaw's gusher started the oil rush here. In just a few years the population was two thousand and growing.

Mrs. Ryan was taking every thing in. Her eyes darted everywhere. She turned to her friend, "Isn't this grand? I have a mind to drill for oil myself."

"You wouldn't!" her friend gasped. She put the handkerchief even tighter against her nose. "It's bad enough having to teach here, but to work in the wells . . ."

Not once did any of them get out of the wagon. They were afraid of ruining their shoes. We took them up to McCabe's well where one man was operating the springboard and whistling at the same time. When he noticed us, he stopped what he was doing. Mrs. Ryan asked him if she could have a try at it. He doffed his hat and told her she was surely welcome to try, but wouldn't she be afraid of ruining her dress.

"Oh, not this old thing." She jumped off of the wagon before anyone could help her. A bit of oil spattered her skirt, but she didn't seem to care. She marched over to the well and asked him how she should work the springboard. He gave her a quick lesson and soon she was working it too. I felt proud of her.

She was so enthusiastic about the drilling that her bonnet fell from her head and rested against her back. The pale sun shone off of her red hair. After a few minutes she thanked the man for his help and got back on the wagon. The bottom of her skirt was oil-soaked and one of the women moved to the other side of the wagon so her own dress wouldn't be ruined.

We drove down Crooked Line, past the shanties where the black families lived. Moses explained who lived there and why.

"How appalling," Mrs. Ryan murmured. The other people averted their eyes.

After some silence Mrs. Ryan piped up, "Do you boys know where the land purchasing office is?"

"I can't rightly say, Ma'am. Do you want me to ask my Uncle Amos?"

"That would be lovely." She smiled at me. At that moment, I swear I liked red hair, though I never had before. Aunt Sadie said red hair was "unseemly," though I suppose it's because a lot of Irish and Scots have it, and Aunt Sadie is English to the bone.

We drew up beside the hotel. I didn't need to help anybody this time because one of the gentlemen got out before me. Mrs. Ryan jumped down before he could help her, but the other two ladies needed assistance.

Before we drove off, Mrs. Ryan said, "You can bring the information when you come to school on Monday. See you then, Titus."

I smiled, but said "fat chance" under my breath. Moses pointed out another group ahead of us at the Oxford. We gave them a tour too. We were pretty busy that day and convinced ourselves it was all right to charge two bits because only the rich could afford to take these tours anyway.

The day would have ended just fine if we hadn't run into John and Max as we brought the last group to Yates General Store. I didn't notice them until it was too late.

CHAPTER

10

I hunched my shoulders so the collar of my coat covered my neck. John had come back from the night shift and was pretty miserable. It's cold working the wells all day. He headed right for Moses and me. Mercy was walking between John and Max. She had a worried look on her face. John spoke first.

"Lookee here. The little half pint. Where's your big brother, boy?"

"Around. And my name's not boy."

"You sure have a strange way of showing respect to your elders . . . boy." He said it with a sneer.

"In order to get respect, you've got to deserve it." I used one of Aunt Sadie's sayings, thinking I was pretty smart in doing it.

In two seconds I found myself pulled off of the wagon and pushed against the clapboard siding of the general store. His breath smelled like the hot fires of Hades. I have to use that word *Hades* because I'm not allowed to use the other word. John must have been drinking moonshine. A Belgian couple living just outside of town sold it to the men who worked the oilrigs.

I turned my face away, the smell was so bad. The veins in his eyes were all bloodshot. My body started to tremble under his huge hand. I was afraid he was going to hit me in the face.

I wasn't wrong because one of his arms drew back to throw a punch at me. I put my hands up to protect my head. Someone called out for him to leave me alone.

"Longville, why don't you pick on someone your own size?"

John grumbled, looked embarrassed, and dropped me to the ground.

"Where's the fiddle and book?" he asked.

Mercy shook her head no at me. "What?" I asked.

"If you don't tell me where the fiddle and book are, I'm taking this lady to the constable and pressing charges of thievery."

This looked pretty serious to me. I wasn't sure who the constable was, and I didn't want to have any trouble with the law.

"What makes you think she stole a fiddle and . . ." Moses asked.

"You shut up. We got no business with the likes of you," John's speech was slurred from the drink, and he was angry.

Max called Moses a coon and told him to get back to Crooked Line where he belonged. I would have spoke up, but Mercy seemed to need my help more. Moses felt the same way as me and stood his ground.

There seemed to be a bruise forming on Mercy's left cheek and Moses went to touch it. "Did they do this to you?"

John flung Moses arm away. "Don't you dare touch a white girl!"

"Or what?" I piped up. Max and John were big, and we could see they had already hurt Mercy, but something made me talk back anyway.

"Or we'll hurt your friends."

Now Max was holding onto Moses and John had Mercy. They moved back into the alley so people wouldn't see them.

"How can I trust you won't hurt them until I get back with the fiddle and book?"

"You can't," Max said.

"Then I won't go," I was being stubborn, but these

were my friends. "Get on the wagon," I told them. "I'll take you home to get the stuff."

"We ain't going anywheres with you. Bring the stuff here."

They assured me they would wait right there, so I rushed home to get the things. Seems Lem was more partial to that fiddle than I thought. He decided to come along with me to teach John a lesson. If Uncle Amos had been there, I'm sure he would have come with us too.

When John and Max saw Lem, they backed up, but they dragged Mercy and Moses with them. The sight of Lem when he's angry is enough to scare anyone.

"Let them go," Lem told them.

They shoved Mercy and Moses into us, then high-tailed it out of there. By the look on John's face as he ran past, I ventured to guess we would be seeing him soon.

We escorted Mercy to the hotel and then took Moses home in the wagon. Lem told Mercy he didn't like the idea of her working in the hotel with the likes of John and Max around. But there was nothing any of us could do because Mercy needed her job. I was especially worried about Moses. Who knew what John was capable of?

CHAPTER

11

Moses and I were out one Sunday, fooling around. We had made these slingshots and were shooting cans at the back of Yates's store. Moses was a pretty darn good shot, and he was showing me how to aim. We used stones or clots of ice or mud as ammunition. It was fun, though I kept losing to Moses. But with practice, I was improving.

We came up to the front of the store to get ourselves a treat, seeing as we'd made a little money that week with our runs. Max was coming up the walk, so we ducked quickly into the store, hoping he hadn't seen us.

We stood behind a shelf of goods watching Max as he spoke with a group of men warming themselves by the stove. I'm sorry to say I don't rightly remember who was there. It didn't seem important at the time.

We eavesdropped as they talked about the "Negro

problem" to the south of us. That meant the people living on Crooked Line. The men claimed the Negroes worked for less than the whites because they wanted to steal the jobs for themselves. Moses had already told me that wasn't true. The Negroes worked for low wages because low wages were all they were offered.

Max said something about how him and John were going to teach those blacks a lesson. I was angry, but I didn't worry too much because they were a bunch of cowards to my way of thinking.

Anyway, we got to funning between ourselves, and I said to Moses, "When he leaves, we should shoot something at him."

Moses looked at me like I was crazy. "What good will that do?"

"I'm not sure, but it's a powerful temptation."

We both stayed there for a minute, crouched behind the shelves. Then I made up my mind. "I'm gonna do it. If we stay hidden, he won't know it's us."

"Yeah, right," Moses rolled his eyes at me. "He's not a complete idiot, you know."

"But think of how good it will feel to hit him. I won't use a stone, just some mud so he won't get hurt."

Instead of mud, I picked up some frozen manure once we were outside. We didn't have to wait very long.

99

As Max left the store, I took aim and got him right between his shoulder blades. Max turned before we could duck behind the corner of the building.

Moses pulled on my sleeve.

"Run, Titus." He dragged me along as he ran. "Don't look back. It'll slow you down."

We ran like the hounds of Hades were after us. After a good number of blocks we stopped, out of breath and hid behind a line of wagons.

"We got rid of him sure enough."

"How?" I asked.

"By running faster than him." Moses started laughing.

"Sh!" I whispered. "Do you want him to find us?"

"Don't look so scared. Do you see him anywhere here?" Moses spread his arms out wide.

We sat down on the ground, tired from the running. I looked up at the wintry sky and saw snow clouds moving in. Flakes started to fall slowly around us. Moses raised his face to the sky too.

"You know something, Moses?" I said. "It felt powerful good to get him like that."

"I bet it did. I kinda wish I was the one that got him."

We both laughed, then. We didn't care if anyone heard us or not. It was good to laugh like that with the snow falling and wetting our faces. Still, I was sure that Max would get back at us somehow for the morning's excitement. Troublemaking was his stock in trade.

"We should get to the wagon." Moses pointed to where a group of people were forming in front of the Oxford. It might be a good day after all.

That night I mentioned to Uncle Amos what I'd overheard in the general store. "Who was he talking to?" Uncle Amos asked.

"I didn't know them," I replied.

"I'm sure John's behind this and . . ." Uncle Amos never completed his sentence, but I could see he was a little disturbed by what I'd told him.

He looked up at the clock on the mantel and said, "It's time to be off to bed, son." So we all turned in and wished for the new house to be done.

CHAPTER

12

With winter there were fewer people to take on a tour of the town, so Moses and I hauled the clay that was left after drilling the wells. We also loaded ash trees and hauled them to the different well sites. We didn't do this work alone: Mr. Croucher helped, and we used his horses. The wagons weren't made for oil runs. You needed a special kind fitted with a barrel lying sideways to hold the oil.

Uncle Amos and Lem would take our horses and deliver the oil barrels to the refinery. It was easier taking oil on the frozen roads. Sledges were used once the snow was on the ground and it made the work a lot easier.

Uncle Amos's house was done and it cost a pretty piece. As Aunt Sadie would say, money ran through everyone's fingers like water. I preferred to think it ran like oil, black and grubby sometimes, slippery other times, but it kept running.

Uncle Amos decided it was time to move in. We swept and cleaned the house that smelled of sawn lumber. There was a hallway that led to the front door with parlors on each side of it. The windows looked out over the road. The kitchen was at back and there were five bedrooms upstairs.

I laughingly asked Uncle Amos what he needed all the space for. Seems he was going back into doctoring. He had his friend, James Wakefield, make a sign, and he hung out his shingle before we moved in. James also made the beds that were in the one front parlor. This was going to be the local hospital. There were constant cases of cholera fever, since the drinking water wasn't as good as it should be. We always had to boil our water before we drank it. The crowded conditions in the hotels didn't help much either.

We were going to have a party before we moved the beds in. Lem was to play the fiddle while Uncle Amos played the guitar. There would be dancing and merrymaking. While we worked at sweeping the place clean, there was a knock on the door. We weren't expecting anyone for a while yet, but when I answered the door, there was Mrs. Ryan, standing on the porch with a book in her hand.

"Well, Titus. I thought I'd find you here. I've come to speak with your uncle."

"Yes, ma'am," I replied. I opened the door wider so she could come in.

"Mr. Sullivan?"

"Yes?"

"I'm Mrs. Ryan, Titus's teacher. Seems he's been truant most days this past month. Is there a reason why he's absent from school?"

Uncle Amos looked at me and I hid a little behind Mrs. Ryan.

"Is this true, Titus?"

"Yes, sir."

"Come from behind your teacher, boyo. There's no hiding behind petticoats."

So I stood in front of my uncle, my face red. I don't suppose there was anything I could say that would make either of them happy.

"He's such a bright pupil, it seems a waste for him not to be in school," Mrs. Ryan said.

"What were you up to when you weren't in school?" Uncle Amos asked.

I told him about the business Moses and I had started. He seemed a little startled. Then he turned to Lem. "Did you know of this?"

It was Lem's turn to be embarrassed. "Yes, sir."

"I wondered why the horses were gone some days. Just assumed you had them, Lem. Mrs. Ryan, I believe Titus and I owe you an apology, and we'll see that he's back in school next week." As an afterthought he added, "I'll speak with you later, Titus."

Well, sir, I was discouraged by this news as you can well imagine. I had provided a service for the village that I thought was more important than sitting in school all day, looking out the window, and wishing I was somewheres else. Mrs. Ryan talked with my uncle awhile longer in the hallway while I continued to sweep.

I didn't rightly know then what they discussed, but I was to find out later that night. They had agreed to let me continue my business two days out of the week, and I would go to school for three days. I would do assignments for Mrs. Ryan and hand them in at the end of the week. She knew that I was ahead of my class, and she was willing to give me private lessons. I was extremely happy when I found that out.

Our dance that night was a festive affair, and many people came throughout the evening. There was dancing in one parlor and eating in the other. We borrowed chairs from neighbors so people had a place to rest in between the dances. Snow fell softly while we were inside. By the end of the party the ground was covered, and it was beautiful with the full moon shining down on all the white stuff.

December passed quickly and with no trouble. We all wondered where John and Max had disappeared to, though no one missed them. Then Tom told us they had been arrested in Sarnia for drunk and disorderly conduct. There was still the occasional grumbling about wages, but all in all, everything seemed fine.

I got a few letters from Aunt Sadie while I was in Oil Springs. Mostly they just told me she was coming at Christmas and that she would take me back to London with her. I talked with Uncle Amos about that, and he was pretty quiet on the subject. Maybe he thought Aunt Sadie was right in wanting me to go back with her. I tried not to worry so I could enjoy the new house more.

I liked all the windows because you could look out and see a good chunk of the whole town, depending where you stood. The shanty had been dark with only two little windows. There was supposed to be some furniture shipped by train from London. Aunt Sadie had picked it out under instructions from Uncle Amos. On Saturday we were all going to go to the town of Wyoming with the sleigh and sledge to pick things up.

Moses and his family were headed back to Chatham for Christmas and would return after a week. One day Moses and I had done a few runs and were reading at our house when Mercy came for a visit.

"Is Lem home?" she asked.

"No," I said, about to close the door. Then I realized how rude that would be. It was cold out, and we had hot tea on the table. I could hear Aunt Sadie's voice in my head, telling me "Invite her in. It's the least you could do."

I admit I sighed and groaned a bit, but I opened the door wide. "Come on in, there's tea."

Mercy followed me through the hallway to the dining room, where we were sitting. "When's he coming then?" she asked.

"What? Who? Oh, Lem. Probably tomorrow."

She hung her shawl on the back of a chair and poured tea for all of us, like it was her own house or something.

"Who makes supper when they're gone?" she asked.

She picked up her cup and sipped some tea as she stood behind Moses looking at his book. Then she turned to me.

"Could you teach me?" she whispered.

I didn't know what she was talking about. Was she asking me to teach her how to cook?

Moses interrupted, "She wants to learn to read, Titus."

"Lem knows how to read too, right?" she asked.

"Yes," I hesitated. "Is that why you want to learn?"

"I guess."

"It's hard work, just ask Moses."

Mercy thought about that for a minute, then she said, "Can we start now?"

I grabbed my school slate and began to teach her right then and there. You see, this proved I didn't need to go to school because I already knew enough to teach someone else. I think I learned even more, teaching her. Seems I could probably have taken over for Mrs. Ryan.

Mercy was a quick learner. When she finally could read, we got to memorizing poetry. That was another thing altogether. Moses found some of the poems just plain silly. He said *Beowulf* was more interesting than talking about "a host of golden daffodils." Mercy didn't agree. She was partial to the poems of Wordsworth. She especially liked "I wandered lonely as a cloud."

"That reminds me of you," she told me. "Even when you're with people you seem lonely."

"What do you mean?" I asked.

"You sort of watch everything with a different look on your face, like you know everything better than us."

That made me sound like I was proud, and I wasn't at all. No, sir. I'm more of a coward as even John Longville could see. When this all started to happen he called me a coward and laughed when I couldn't talk back.

Seems Mercy wanted to quit working for her aunt. Because none of us appeared to like housework, it was easy convincing Uncle Amos to hire her. She got one of the extra bedrooms upstairs and made sure we had food to eat and that the house was kept neat. She even cleaned the hospital rooms. Someone else came in to do the laundry.

It was December 23, almost Christmas. Aunt Sadie and Uncle Robert were coming on the train. Lem thought he would borrow Tom's sleigh to pick them up in the morning. Moses had already left with his family for Chatham with the promise he would return in the New Year.

I cleaned a patch of frost off the window that morning so I could look outside. I was real nervous about seeing Aunt Sadie, so I wished I could stay in Oil Springs while Lem went to get them. I went on down to the store to pick up some provisions while Mercy was blacking the stove.

At the store I looked over the potatoes and picked the nicer ones, the way Aunt Sadie taught me. I heard someone clear her throat behind me and turned to see Miss Ryan at my elbow. Her eyes were twinkling and she asked me if I had any plans for Christmas.

I told her about my aunt and uncle coming from London. Then I asked her if she was heading home for Christmas.

"This is my home now," she pointed down the street.

"Did you buy a house?" I asked.

"Yes I did."

"Do you have family coming for Christmas ma'am?" I asked.

"Heavens no." She smiled at that. "They think I'm crazy for living here."

"Why do you want to be here ma'am? I don't mean to be impertinent."

She waved her arms as if shooing a fly away from her. "Don't worry young man. I like it here. I like the rough and tumble way of life. It suits me fine."

"Have you drilled a well, or do you have a well on your property?" I asked.

"Not yet. But I'll strike a gusher. I'll bet my bottom dollar on it," she wrapped a scarf around her bonnet and headed for the door. I stood holding potatoes in my hand until I finally remembered my manners.

"If you're alone for Christmas, you could come and spend the day with us."

She turned then, a smile lighting her face. But the smile didn't linger. She looked at me, serious-like. "You should check with your family first, Titus, before you ask a guest. Your uncle might not take it too kindly."

"I don't suppose Uncle Amos would mind all that much, but Mercy might," I replied thoughtfully.

"Is she cooking the Christmas goose?"

"Yes, but she was complaining a little this morning about having to cook everything by herself."

"Have you bought the goose yet?"

"Uncle Amos is killing one as we speak."

"What do you say we go now after you get your provisions? I need to speak with your uncle about your schooling."

I wondered if I had done something wrong, but wasn't about to ask, seeing as I was so nervous that I dropped the potatoes on the floor. She bent down and picked them up, putting them gently back in my arms.

We lugged the groceries home and put everything in the kitchen before looking out back for Uncle Amos. He had slaughtered the goose and was busy plucking it.

When we reached him I said, "I invited Mrs. Ryan for Christmas dinner, seeing as she'll be alone."

I hoped that would distract her from talking about my schoolwork. I just remembered an essay I was supposed to hand in and hadn't got finished yet.

Uncle Amos looked at both of us kind of funny-like, and then he smiled at Mrs. Ryan and me. "A pleasure I'm sure," he said. "I hope you like stuffed goose."

"Who doesn't?" I piped up.

"Do you need help with the plucking?" Mrs. Ryan asked my uncle.

"Now ma'am that wouldn't be a fitting way to treat a guest would it?" Uncle Amos joked. "But Titus can put a kettle on so we can all have tea when I've finished here."

"That'll will be fine," Mrs. Ryan lifted her skirt slightly to keep it out of the wet snow as she walked back to the house.

"Titus." Uncle Amos said it softly so only I would hear. I went to him. "You sure you want your teacher here for dinner?"

"Yes. She's pretty nice, and she's a good teacher most of the time."

Uncle Amos smiled. "It was thoughtful of you to think of someone else at Christmas."

I waited to see if he had anything more to say, but he didn't. I followed Mrs. Ryan into the house. She had just put some water in the kettle and put it on the stove.

"This house doesn't look too much like Christmas does it?" she said, turning to me.

"We just moved in, ma'am, and not all the furniture has come yet. There's some coming tomorrow with my aunt and uncle."

"Why don't we go out to the woods to see if we can borrow some evergreen boughs?"

It was kind of nice the way she pretended the trees were like people and might give us permission to take a branch of two off of them. It was good to find someone else with an imagination in this town.

"I know where there is a very kind tree, one that just loves Christmas," I played right along with her.

We laughed together as we gathered boughs and the bittersweet that grew along a fencerow. Back home, we put the boughs on the mantle and scattered the bitter-sweet amongst them. It looked real pretty. The rest of the bittersweet went into a vase on the big table.

By the time we finished, the goose was plucked and in the pantry under a clean tea towel. Mercy was back in the kitchen making pies and the tea had been poured. Uncle Amos got out his pipe and went to the corner cupboard for his tobacco. Mercy shooed me to the root cellar to fetch some apples. By the time I came back, Uncle Amos was smoking comfortably on a kitchen chair, reading a book. Mrs. Ryan looked relaxed sitting across the table from him. She took the apples from me and began peeling them while Mercy worked on the pastry.

I sat down to help with the apples. I didn't mind one bit because Mrs. Ryan never told me to do it. She's not bossy like Mercy. I found myself talking to her about things, just the way I do with Uncle Amos. Once I caught his eye on me, and he was grinning. I was probably talking too much and tried to be quiet, but the words just came out. I told her about Moses and me and our business, and I told her about John Longville.

"You don't like him?" she asked me.

"No, ma'am," I solemnly replied.

"Well then he must be a no-good bounder, and I won't like him either." There was a little bit of laughter in her voice, but I knew she was kind of serious too. Uncle Amos pretended to ignore us, but I knew he wasn't reading because he hadn't turned a page for the past five minutes.

Mercy was getting kind of angry with me because she said I was in the way and I was talking too much, so I left the kitchen. I heard her slip the pies into the oven.

Suddenly, it felt like home here, and just as suddenly I wished Mrs. Ryan was my mother and Uncle Amos was my father. The slam of the oven door scattered my thoughts and my childish dream vanished. I leaned my head against the window and hoped Lem would come home from work soon.

Mrs. Ryan ended up staying for a supper of bean soup with homemade biscuits. Uncle Amos thought it would be fine to have some of the wine we had saved up for Christmas. It glowed in the glasses I had shined just before filling them. I was given only a sip or two from my uncle's glass because I was too young, as Aunt Sadie would say, to imbibe.

I wasn't sleepy as I got ready for bed that night. I was afraid and excited at the same time. I was afraid Aunt Sadie would take me back with her, and I was excited about getting presents. Not only that, Uncle Amos had started calling Mrs. Ryan by her first name – Isabelle – some time during the evening. To my way of thinking that was a good sign. So it took a mite longer to get to sleep that night.

CHAPTER

13

Aunt Sadie and Uncle Robert came in on the morning train. We were out bright and early to get them. I had decided to go in the sleigh after all, the one that Lem was in charge of. Uncle Amos had the sledge so we could pick up the furniture at the same time. I sang every Christmas carol I knew, even though Lem told me to shut up once or twice.

"Leave the boy be," Uncle Amos said as he slapped the reins on the horses' rumps. "It's a beautiful sound on a morning such as this."

Once or twice Uncle Amos joined in, but the closer we got to Wyoming, the quieter I got. I was worried about Aunt Sadie, and I don't mind saying so. She had the power to ruin my life. Oil Springs was my home now. I never wanted to return to London and I had said as much to Uncle Amos that morning. He just nodded his head and kept making breakfast.

We didn't have long to wait at the station before the train came down the track. Uncle Amos must have known what I was feeling because he came to stand beside me and put his big hand on my shoulder.

"You've grown, boy," he said, as if he was amazed. He took me by the shoulders and made me face him. "By Jove, you have grown. Why didn't I see it before? Did you get some inches on you just last night?"

I could tell he was joking about growing overnight, but I was taller than when I came because I didn't have to crook my neck so high to look him in the eye.

It felt real good knowing I was getting taller, and I wondered if Aunt Sadie would notice. I suppose that was a stupid thing to wonder because nothing ever escaped her notice. In fact, it was the first thing she said when she got off the train. She came directly at me and pulled me hard against her.

"Why, Titus! You've grown a full six inches I bet." Then she took me by the shoulders and pushed me away from her so she could get a good look. "I swear you're going to be another handsome Sullivan."

Her laughter was a happy sound and I was surprised that she thought we Sullivans were handsome. The men all shook hands. Aunt Sadie turned to Lem and gave him a big hug too.

"It's wonderful to see you all," she said and then sniffed.

I just hoped she wouldn't cry. That was the worse thing she could do, but she got a hold of herself and smiled while she took a small white hankie to dab at her eyes.

A porter brought their bags and we loaded them up. Then we worked to tie down the furniture on the sledge, and we were off back to home. Aunt Sadie's cheerfulness faded the closer we got to Oil Springs. I could see the town through her eyes, and it didn't look like much. There were shanties everywhere, and people were dressed roughly. There was no use dressing up in this place because of the muck and oil.

But, when Aunt Sadie saw the house, she looked less discouraged. She remarked that it was quite suitable for a doctor, and Uncle Amos should go back to being one, instead of running away from responsibility and living like a pauper. She figured God didn't give out talents to be wasted and that Uncle Amos would want to be called a good and faithful servant by God when his time came to die.

Uncle Amos told her that he figured God wasn't all

that concerned – there were enough doctors in the world already.

"Show me all these doctors," Aunt Sadie said. "I suppose they're coming out of the woodwork. Why look, there's a few walking down the street right now."

She pointed at the two town drunks, Henry Wren and Simon Finch. They were stumbling down the road because they were full of moonshine. The townsfolk called them *those rare birds* on account of their last names and all.

We couldn't help but laugh at that. Aunt Sadie sniffed and said it weren't funny that a grown man should make such a meager thing of his life when God had given him so much. Uncle Amos wasn't smiling anymore. I suppose he realized he should tell her the truth.

"Oh hush up, Sadie. As you can see the shingle is hanging by the front door."

Sadie clapped her hands with happiness. "It's about time you came to your senses." Her smile took the sting out of her words.

"You two help with the furniture," Uncle Amos told Lem and me.

With four men it didn't take long to haul it all into the house with Aunt Sadie clucking behind us that we were tracking in snow and dirt. Mercy stood in the doorway, stunned at the sight of Aunt Sadie. She is a whirlwind for sure, and I don't think Mercy knew what to make of her.

After supper we all went to attend the Christmas Eve service at the Methodist church. It was a clapboard structure with a belfry, but no bell as yet. We bundled up for the cold weather and walked the few blocks. Lem took up the rear with Mercy. It seemed sad that Mercy didn't want to spend Christmas with her family, but I didn't blame her since Mrs. Mabee is not a good, truthful kind of person. I wouldn't trust anything she said. Well sir, at least Mercy had us.

There were lots of lonely people at Christmas because many of the men had left their families behind so they could work here. People came and went. Some lost money. Some struck oil. Some hauled oil. Some stayed and settled down. Some came from the south where the civil war was being fought. Some colored, some white. Some brought their ideas about slavery with them and others brought their ideas about freedom. Some were farmers, some were merchants, but all were dreamers who wanted to strike oil. Everyone came together at that little crossroads in Enniskillen Township.

CHAPTER

14

That Christmas was the best ever. Mrs. Ryan had a way of bringing joy into the house; she even charmed Aunt Sadie. All around our large clapboard house there were shanties. The shacks of the Negroes on Crooked Line were even worse. I wondered how they all would keep warm during the winter months. If it was up to me I would have invited them to our place for Christmas, but most of them had gone back to Kent County anyway.

Aunt Sadie would have been very upset to find out that Moses and me were friends. She would have found our friendship inappropriate. It's a good thing Uncle Amos didn't set much store on what people called appropriate and inappropriate. He figured a man should be judged on his deeds, not the color of his skin.

My best gift was a toboggan that Uncle Amos had made. It was pretty heavy, but it worked fine on the freshly fallen snow. Mercy thought she would go with me for a few runs down the hill. Lem decided he would stay at the house. I could tell she was disappointed but she also wanted a turn on the toboggan.

There were a lot of people out, seeing as it was a nice winter day and the wind was not blowing at all. We got to the hill soon enough and watched those who came afore us. My scarf (thanks to Aunt Sadie) was wrapped tightly around my throat. Mercy looked really nice in the new red coat we gave her for Christmas. It was our way of thanking her for all the work she was doing.

Mercy and I did a few runs down the hill, but it was always me lugging the toboggan back up the hill. I guess she figured she was a lady. After three or four runs I looked up and there was Lem, watching as we struggled to haul the toboggan.

"Lem, take Mercy for a ride," I coaxed him, when we got to the top.

"She can go with you." Lem said. I didn't want to kick up a fuss in case Mercy would be even more embarrassed. It seemed pretty obvious to me that I wasn't the brother she wanted to be sliding hills with.

"Come on then," Mercy said in her bossy way. She

grabbed the rope from my hand and told me to sit on the front.

"No." I was firm on that. She could sit in front of me. I didn't want to feel like a little boy with her. She was smaller than me.

She plopped onto the toboggan so hard it started to slide down the hill before I could get on. I made a dive and got on in time. We were flying again and it felt real good.

"Do you want to go down one more time?" I asked her at the bottom of the hill.

Mercy was watching Lem's retreating back. Her eyes narrowed. "No Titus, I don't."

So the two of us trudged through the snow each holding a part of the rope, attached to the toboggan. Lem's long legs had quickly taken him home. We followed more slowly as if Mercy dreaded entering the house. I wasn't sure why Lem had acted so rude and I didn't know how to ask Mercy.

"He didn't mean to hurt you," I said without thinking.

Mercy blushed. She pulled her collar up around her neck and hitched her scarf higher to hide her face.

"He didn't," was all she said.

Lem was on the fiddle when we entered the back door. Uncle Amos had his squeeze box, and Uncle Robert was playing the spoons. Aunt Sadie and Mrs. Ryan sat quietly drinking store-bought tea and eating the cake that Isabelle had made. Mrs. Ryan's toe was tapping to the lively music, but Aunt Sadie sat straight in her chair. There was a bit of melted snow on the floor from our boots, so I got a rag and cleaned it up before Aunt Sadie noticed. Mrs. Ryan smiled, but Aunt Sadie only nodded. The men seemed to be enjoying themselves and paid us no mind.

Mercy went into the kitchen to prepare the meal. There was some whiskey in the glasses that were passed around, but Aunt Sadie only took a little of her own currant cordial because she claimed she abstained from the evils of alcohol. I had become pretty good at step dancing when Lem played the fiddle. I could also play the penny whistle to the old tunes.

I ran up the stairs to get it while the music came to a stop downstairs. The men must have needed a break because when I came back down they were taking sips of their drink. Mrs. Ryan had gone to the other parlor to help set the table. For some strange reason Aunt Sadie followed.

The door to the room was closed. I stood very quiet outside it because I heard my name mentioned and then Mercy's. Aunt Sadie was talking. "Does Titus often go about with this girl, Mercy?"

"I'm not sure, though I have seen them together on occasion," was the reply.

I moved closer to the door. Luckily it was slightly ajar, or I may not have heard all of the conversation.

"I'm not sure an impressionable young boy like him should be associating with the hired help," Aunt Sadie's voice carried her disdain.

There was a pause. I wondered if Mrs. Ryan was as angry as me, or just trying to answer Aunt Sadie's question as best she could. I could feel the blood rush to my head.

"She's a hard-working girl, and I've heard no ill of her."

"I don't suppose you're the type to listen to gossip anyway," Aunt Sadie mused out loud. She was trying to win Mrs. Ryan over by flattering her.

"Well no, but I have never heard anything to discredit Mercy."

I wondered where Mercy was. Maybe she had gone to the privy.

Aunt Sadie said one last thing before I returned to the parlor, forgetting why I had come here in the first place.

"Amos is the most unlikely guardian of any child, but he seems to have taken a shine to his nephew, though I can't begin to wonder why. Amos used to be such a recluse, and now I find him having Christmas with friends and family. I shouldn't wonder that his influence would be inappropriate. He never much cared for the proprieties of life. He always balked at the niceties and formalities. What my sister ever saw in him –"

The back door slammed, and both women stopped speaking. Mercy must have come back into the house.

I turned and glided down the hallway back to the music. My heart was beating fast. I knew Aunt Sadie was going to try to get me to come home with her, even though she didn't even like me. I think she felt she should do her duty. In Aunt Sadie's world, duty was everything.

I hoped that Uncle Amos would stand up for me and keep me with him. He was a good guardian, the best ever, despite what Aunt Sadie said. Mrs. Ryan might have defended Uncle Amos too, if Mercy hadn't come into the kitchen at that moment.

CHAPTER

15

"Pass the potatoes please," Lem asked as we were all seated at the large table. I passed them to him as talk swirled around me. I wasn't really listening because I was worried about Aunt Sadie taking me back to London. I tried to think of a way to talk everyone into letting me stay. I just knew Aunt Sadie was going to bring up the subject while we were eating together. Aunt Sadie never seemed afraid of anyone or anything. In that way I admired her. Her courage was something to respect.

"Where is your school young man? I hope within walking distance?" Aunt Sadie asked, her eyebrows raised.

"Yes," I mumbled, hoping she would drop the subject.

"Is he a good student?" she asked Mrs. Ryan.

"Oh yes, quite the brightest lad in the whole school," Mrs. Ryan replied.

"That is, when he's there," Lem opened his big mouth.

"What do you mean?"

"He works, ma'am." Mercy was trying to help, but I wished she had kept quiet. I kicked at her shin under the table. I couldn't reach Lem or he would have gotten a good kick too.

"At what, pray tell?" Aunt Sadie's voice became louder.

"He helps haul away the clay as new wells are dug. He also drives tourists around to see the sights in Oil Springs."

"The sights!" Aunt Sadie harrumphed. "It's nothing but a muddy, smelly town with too many rough characters in it. Just walking along the main street I came across so many men spitting. They all seem to have acquired the filthy habit of chewing tobacco. Is that what you want for Titus?"

"I'm making money, Aunt Sadie," I piped up. "I'm saving for college like you wanted."

"I never asked you to save for anything. You need an education to attend college, young man. Working as a teamster isn't what I had in mind for your education.

Your Uncle Robert and I were going to pay for your college. It's the least I could do for my sister."

Aunt Sadie took out a small handkerchief and wiped her eyes. I was afraid her tears would do more damage to my cause than anything.

I looked at Uncle Amos with pleading eyes. Mrs. Ryan smiled at me encouragingly when I caught her eye. Mercy stared at her plate. She figured she'd done enough talking for now. Or at least that's what I thought until she ruined everything by saying something else.

"He's helping me learn to read, ma'am. He's a mighty fine teacher. Moses helps to teach too, since he got learning at that school down there in Buxton. He's a right smart reader too, just like Titus, and he puts so much into his reading, it's like hearing the voices of the people he's reading about."

"Who is this Moses?"

There was a deathly silence. We all knew that Aunt Sadie would definitely not approve of Moses. I looked at Uncle Amos in mute appeal. He smiled grimly and answered his sister-in-law.

"He's a boyo that Titus has been chumming with."

"Where does he come from?" Aunt Sadie was not going to be easy to deter.

"Moses comes from Chatham," I replied.

"What's he doing here, then?"

"He travels with his family for work."

"What's that supposed to mean, young man? Is his father a tinker?"

"Just a man wanting to make a living for his family," Uncle Amos put in. "If you insist on knowing, I will tell you that this young man's father was a slave."

Aunt Sophie was aghast. "It's fine and dandy to be an abolitionist, but mingling with these people is going beyond the call of true Christian duty."

I was very angry then as you can imagine. I see myself as a Christian, and the abolitionists are definitely doing God's work, so what my Aunt said didn't make any sense. She looked at Uncle Amos plaintively. "How could you so disgrace my sister's memory?"

Once again the handkerchief came out, and she dabbed at her eyes. Uncle Robert came to stand behind her and lay a hand on her shoulder. "Do you think it's wise?" he asked my uncle.

"You never cared what any of us ever thought of you. You always went your own way, defying the rules of society." Aunt Sadie was gasping now, and the tears were flowing fast. "It's fine for you to defy authority, you're a grown man, but the boy . . . the boy . . ."

Aunt Sadie couldn't finish her sentence she was so

distraught. Uncle Robert kept squeezing her shoulder while the rest of us sat, staring dumbly at our plates. Mercy was the first to get up and excuse herself.

"The dishes won't get done on their own, I daresay," she said, picking up the empty plates. Her chair scraped against the new wood floor and she moved quickly to leave the room. Mrs. Ryan followed.

When the two were in the kitchen Aunt Sadie recovered from crying. "Now then, I see that I should take Titus back with me."

She got up from the table all businesslike as if she was leaving right then and there. I cringed in my chair. Uncle Amos seemed composed at first, but the longer I looked at him the grimmer his face became. Then, he got up too.

"You, dear sister-in-law, will do nothing of the sort," he said those words through clenched teeth.

I was spellbound by what was happening. I wanted to believe that right would win out in the end, and as far as I was concerned, Uncle Amos would always be in the right over Aunt Sadie.

"You have proven yourself incapable of watching over him," Aunt Sadie placed her hands on the table, leaned forward, and stared at him. "Who looks after him when you do your runs to Sarnia?"

"He stays here."

"Alone?" Aunt Sadie acted appalled. "How dare you leave a child alone?"

"He's not alone, Aunt Sadie," Lem interrupted. "Tom sometimes stays with him, and Mercy is here too."

"A mere child with a child," Aunt Sadie was not impressed by that.

"I'm not doing runs after Christmas," Lem continued, "so, I'll be here most of the time too."

"Most of the time? Well, that's not good enough. In a town of rough men, you dare leave my nephew alone?" Aunt Sadie was screeching now. "He's a child for heaven's sake!"

I didn't move in my seat in case Aunt Sadie noticed and turned her anger my way.

"The child needs a father *and* a mother, something you can't supply." Aunt Sadie was triumphant. There was no disputing the fact that Uncle Amos was unmarried.

"You would coddle him too much. He's grown up in the short time he's been here. He's becoming responsible for himself."

"He's not a man yet, Amos. He still has years to go before then. I agreed to Lem living here, but I never gave permission for Titus –"

"Granted, that's true." Uncle Amos sighed and

covered his eyes for a moment. Uncle Robert remained silent as if none of this was his business.

"We made the best of it when he came," Lem was sticking up for Uncle Amos. "He goes to school some of the time and writes essays and such. You should read them, Aunt Sadie. They're really good. Ask Mrs. Ryan. I think Titus would make a fine writer."

"He was *supposed* to be a lawyer." Aunt Sadie made it all sound so final, my future and everything.

"What if I don't want to be a lawyer?" I asked in a squeaky voice, but no one took any notice of me.

Mrs. Ryan and Mercy were still in the kitchen. I took some more plates from the table and joined them while the argument swirled in the dining room. Mercy took the plates when I entered the room.

I walked over to Mrs. Ryan and threw my arms around her waist. I was crying and didn't even know it until my tears fell freely on her apron. She patted my back a few times. We stood like that until I stopped sobbing. "I don't want to leave. I'll miss everyone. . . ."

"Hush child. Hush."

A powerful feeling filled me. Crying wasn't going to do much good. I needed Aunt Sadie to see and understand that I belonged here. I needed to convince her that I should stay. It was up to me to say my piece.

I straightened my shoulders, smiled at Mrs. Ryan and wiped away the remaining tears. I turned around and headed back to the dining room. The argument was loud and heated now. Mean things were being said by both my uncle and aunt.

"I'm staying, Aunt Sadie," I shouted, trying to be heard over their loud voices.

They continued to yell. I tugged on Aunt Sadie's skirt. She turned around, her face red and eyes glaring.

"What do you want? Go pack your bags. We're leaving this instant! I will not spend another night under the roof of this house!"

"I'm staying. If you don't want me to be alone when Uncle Amos does his runs, I can stay with Mrs. Ryan, I'm sure. You might find this town rough, but the people are good to each other. I have made friends and I work hard. I study too, Aunt Sadie. I can show you the essays I wrote. I also study science and am learning the process of distilling the oil. I watch Lem when he makes new hooks for the jerker lines. I am learning so much . . ."

I said a lot more to her then. She was quiet the whole time I was talking. It was like her anger had gone out of her. Finally I was done.

"Fine. I tried my best. I let you stay here against my better judgment, thinking you would be ready to come home after Christmas. But no, you're an ungrateful boy. You want to be selfish and destroy your future? Go ahead." She turned to my uncle. "Robert, we're leaving in fifteen minutes, just as soon as I pack our bags."

Uncle Robert followed Aunt Sadie. Later, the three of us admitted we felt a little ashamed that we had hurt her so much. But, Uncle Amos had fought to keep me here. This was like a song in my heart. I was loved and needed – and it had nothing to do with duty.

CHAPTER

16

A few days passed and Aunt Sadie and Uncle Robert were still in town while they waited for someone to give them a ride to the train station in Wyoming. They stayed at one of the hotels where Uncle Robert was able to get them a room.

In the meantime I was trying my darndest to bring Mrs. Ryan and Uncle Amos together, but that was more for me than them. I really liked my teacher and thought she would be a good person to have around to take the rough edges off of us Sullivan men. Besides, she liked adventure as much as the rest of us. I knew that if Mrs. Ryan married my uncle, I would have a mother, and Aunt Sadie would have a harder time getting me away from Uncle Amos.

Uncle Amos finally decided that he would take Aunt Sadie and Uncle Robert to Wyoming so they could catch the train. He wanted Lem and me to go with him, since it was a family affair. I dreaded seeing Aunt Sadie because I thought she would still be angry.

Uncle Robert was in the lobby reading a paper. When he looked up over the edge of it to see me, his eyes appeared to be smiling. That gave me the courage to go up to him.

"Hello Uncle Robert, sir," I said with a smile.

Lem reached around me to shake Uncle Robert's hand. "Boys, good of you to come." His voice was hearty. "Your Aunt Sadie is overseeing the final details of packing up. I daresay she'll be down shortly."

He pulled his pocketwatch from his vest and studied it for a few seconds. By this time, Uncle Amos had joined us. The two men greeted each other, and Uncle Robert offered Uncle Amos a cheroot. They sat down companionably and lit their cigars.

We didn't talk much while we waited for my aunt to come down the stairs. I was the first to notice her. She sailed through the lobby in her bombazine dress as if she owned the place. One thing about Aunt Sadie is that she has what people call presence. I supposed that comes from being born to quality.

We Sullivans were just dirt farmers from Ireland. It was still a puzzlement to my aunt that her sister, my ma, married my pa. It were no puzzlement to me because Pa was a good man with laughter in his voice. He was a loving father and played the fiddle so well it was enough to make one weep, at least that's what Uncle Amos said.

I try hard to remember things about my parents, but sometimes I forget and feel guilty because they've only been dead about a year. Other times, just before I fall asleep, I see them clear-like and hear them as if they were in the room with me. Those are special times for me, and I hoard them like treasures.

"I see you are on time. I thank you kindly, Amos."

Aunt Sadie's words were nice enough but her tone wasn't. It was cold and crimped-like. I could tell she was controlling her temper, something fierce. Uncle Amos studied the smoke that spiraled around his head before he answered. He was controlling his anger too.

"No thanks needed, Sadie. You're family." His voice was gruff.

Lem got up quickly from his chair and offered it to her. Aunt Sadie sat down with a huff. She leaned forward in her seat and whispered to Uncle Amos, "Don't think I've given up yet. But I'll make a concession. You send that boy to school full time, and I won't bother you about him until summer."

Uncle Amos eyebrows rose at these words. "That

long eh?" He smiled to take the sharpness out of his words, but Aunt Sadie was having none of it.

"I was appointed guardian, and I can take you to court," she threatened.

"Now, now Sadie," Uncle Robert leaned over to touch her knee. "Let's not do anything rash."

"Fine for you to say. I'm a woman who has always taken my duty seriously. I promised to see that Titus finishes his education. I always keep my word."

She was dabbing at her eyes again. Truth be told I was getting heartily sick of her crying. Uncle Amos stubbed out his cheroot and leaned toward Aunt Sadie.

"The boy will go to school full time. I promise you that."

I was disgusted. There's nothing like tears to make a man agree with a woman. Aunt Sadie nodded, sniffed, and wiped her eyes one more time. She put away the scrap of lace in her reticule and snapped it shut. "That's that then. I suppose we should be on our way. Some colorful character said there's a storm on the way."

"A colorful character?" Lem hooted. "The town's full of them." He picked up their suitcases and led the way out of the hotel to the waiting sleigh.

The ride to Wyoming was beautiful and uneventful. The sunlight made the snow sparkle like diamonds as it sifted and flew from under the sleigh's runners. There wasn't hint of a storm at all and I supposed Aunt Sadie just said that to be ornery and contrary.

She sat in the back with me and Lem. She was on the other side of Lem so I didn't pay her no mind for a good part of the trip. The air was frigid, and my face was numb. I stomped my feet a few times to get some life in them. Sharp pains ran through my feet and almost made me cry out.

None of us said much on the trip because there wasn't much to say. Uncle Amos sat hunched over against the cold and I could tell by the set of his back he was not in a good temper. Uncle Robert made some commonplace statements about the snow and cold, but other than that, the swish of runners and the jingle of the harness were the only sounds we made.

At the station the good-byes were quick and to the point. We could already hear the whistle of the train in the distance. Within five minutes it was there, and we helped my aunt and uncle onto it. The porter was a black man and I wondered if he had escaped from the south. I smiled at him as I handed him one of the valises. He smiled back and touched the brim of his cap.

Uncle Amos relaxed on the way home. I could tell from his back, so I ventured to ask a question or two.

"Uncle Amos, how come Aunt Sadie don't like you none?"

"Titus, that's not a fair question. Besides, what makes you think that?"

"Well you two never seem to agree on anything, and she doesn't want me staying with you."

"It's not unusual for a woman to think a bachelor is incapable of looking after a young boy."

"But it makes the most sense, since you were a boy once yourself."

"So was Uncle Robert. If you stayed with Aunt Sadie you would have the benefit of a woman's kindly touch too."

Saying Aunt Sadie was kind was really just hogwash as far as I could figure. Amos had more kindness in his pinkie finger than she had in her whole person. I was about to say something like that when Lem shot me a warning look. My brother knew me too well. But I didn't think Uncle Amos was given enough credit for doing a good job of looking after me.

"I know she thinks you're not doing a good job, but I disagree."

"Not good enough, Titus. I think she was right when she said I should send you back to school full time. You did a mighty fine job writing essays for me, but in the New Year you'll be attending school every day with children more your age."

"But what about my job?" I wailed.

"You'd think you were sending him to the gallows the way he's carrying on," Lem joked.

I sat still for a minute or two because I was angry. But then, the anger went away and left me sad.

"Uncle Amos?"

"What, son?"

"How come I'm feeling a mite sorry for Aunt Sadie right about now? You figure that I would just feel happy about staying. But, this sadness keeps interrupting my happiness and I regret I had to hurt her to stay with you."

"That's life, son. You will never make everyone happy, no matter how hard you try. People are always seeing the same things in a different light, and well . . . people are just plain contrary."

I leaned against my uncle's shoulder for a while. I was drawing from his strength, even though he seemed to be disagreeing with me. He put his pipe in his mouth and patted my hand that rested on his shoulder. The smoke was a thin spiral above his head.

"Look over yonder," he whispered.

There were five bucks, the oldest leading the way over the tree-lined road. The leader had a huge rack, but the other four were young and their antlers were small.

"Too bad we didn't bring the gun," Lem whispered back. "There's meat for the winter."

"I'm glad," I said. "I wouldn't want anyone to shoot them."

I spoke too loud for the big stag lifted his head and looked around until he spotted us. Lem stopped the sleigh while we watched each one run and jump and disappear into the forest.

CHAPTER

17

It was a week before Moses's family made it back. In that time we managed to move Uncle Amos's small house to Crooked Line. We used two teams of horses and logs to roll it over there. Rocks and stumps made the foundation, and we laid straw around the bottom of the house to keep it warm for them. Uncle Amos, Lem, and Adam McCabe took a week off to do this. Mr. McCabe had returned from London after leaving his wife there with her mother. They never had any children, so I suppose Mr. McCabe was a mite lonesome. He seemed to take a shine to me because he used to tease me something fierce, but there was no meanness in it.

Mercy cleaned the shanty, and we installed the Crouchers' woodstove in it. It was my idea of a surprise for them, seeing that Mr. Croucher was so busy working he didn't have much time to fix up his home.

Then I had doubts that maybe we had moved too quickly doing this. What if we offended them? I knew they were a family with dignity, and they might look on our gift as charity, instead of simple neighborliness. It really wasn't much of a house anyway and it would have just rotted in our front yard. Turns out I worried for nothing. When the Crouchers returned they were as pleased as punch.

Winter kept up with snowstorms and frozen temperatures. The going was pretty good for taking oil to Wyoming or Sarnia, and Amos was out a lot with the team. I attended school and found it wasn't so bad, though I missed Moses something bad.

The colored folk worked hard wherever they could find work. Moses and his pa cut down ash trees or hauled wood if they weren't hauling clay from the wells. At the store there was still grumbling 'bout the coloreds working for less pay. I figured it could all have been taken care of if the bosses just paid them the same as the white folk.

When I told Moses what I thought he replied, "That is a good idea, but who is going to convince the bosses that we are worth as much as the whites?"

I spent a good part of that winter just being plain sick. I seemed to catch a cold so easily and often I had stomach upsets. Uncle Amos said it was due to the water not being quite right. The water got mixed with the oil sometimes, and it didn't always taste so good. Uncle Amos blamed the cholera epidemic on the drinking water and had always told me I had to boil it before I drank it. I tried my best to do that, but sometimes I was real thirsty and didn't bother. Mrs. Ryan came one day to ask why I wasn't at school. She could see that I was sick when I opened the door. But other than that, the winter passed by all right. In all this time I never saw so much as a hair on John Longville's head. Max McQuarrie was also nowhere to be found. I figured after they got out of jail they must've been in Sarnia, maybe working on the ships or something. We'd hear rumors about them, but that was all.

When spring finally did come and the frost left the ground, the earth was mucky again. It was very hard to get the oil to the refineries. It also was powerful hard trying to keep anything clean. Lemuel laid a wooden sidewalk to our door. He built it with Tom and me on a quiet afternoon. The cold was still there and it froze up the fingers when you were nailing the boards. He made his own nails and made sure I didn't waste any when I helped with hammering. I only hit my finger once and that was enough because it's pretty hard working with frozen fingers plus one that's purple from the swelling. Still and all, we were pretty proud of that sidewalk.

One morning when I was feeling poorly, I went down to the kitchen to watch Mercy work. Anything was better than being in my bedroom. It almost felt like a jail cell, no offense intended.

"Everyone is getting sick," she said as she tied an apron around her waist. She had spent the day in the sick room with Uncle Amos. After washing her hands, she began to peel potatoes for supper. "Don't you get near me," she warned when I stood next to her.

"It's nothing much," I said through my stuffed nose. "Just a little cold."

"Then why are people dying?" she asked. "I saw a whole bunch of coffins outside the hotel this morning. They shipped them in from London because Mr. Whelan can't keep up."

Mr. Whelan was the local cooper and he also made coffins, when someone died. This scared me something fierce. I thought it was just a cold. Maybe I would die just like my parents. I could feel the water entering my eyes and my nose started running. I wiped it on the sleeve of my nightshirt.

"Don't do that. It's not very nice." Mercy got a handkerchief out of a drawer and handed it to me. "Maybe you should ask your uncle to put you in the sick room."

"I've been in bed all night. I want to go outside."

"Well, you can't. So stop whining."

"I'm not whining. It's just so boring sitting here all day."

"Why don't you read to me while I get the washtubs ready."

I could tell she really wanted me to do that. It made the time pass quicker if she was thinking on a story.

"I like the way you read. You make everything sound so exciting."

I was about to look in the parlor for a book, but she surprised me and pulled a penny novel out of the pocket of her apron. "I brought something myself."

She handed it to me. I knew this book was just a packet of lies and not very adventurous because Uncle Amos said penny novels were trash.

"I could read you about the soldiers down south," I volunteered hopefully, but she would have none of it.

"Do the soldiers down south have ghosts and mansions and a man and woman falling in love? Do they have dark nights with the moon shining down and sinister villains?"

"No, but they have adventure and real life hardship," I retorted.

"I have real life hardship already. I want something different when I read."

"Well I'll be reading, not you," I argued.

"Yes, because you read so well." She was trying to butter me up with her soft talk. Though I'd been teaching her, she didn't want to admit she still couldn't read well enough to get through the whole book by herself. Most of the words were too big and there were no pictures to guide her along. I supposed Uncle Amos didn't need to know what we were reading. He would be disappointed if he saw me with one of those penny novels.

So I gave in, and we spent the morning in the kitchen with me reading, and Mercy working. She had strong arms for a girl. She put the kettle on the stove to heat up after several trips to the backyard to pump the water. I offered to bring some of the buckets in, but she wouldn't let me because I was sick.

"I am not going to be responsible for your death." Her hands rested on her hips as she glared at me.

I rolled my eyes and sat down. I was surprised to find the story interesting. I helped to hang the clothing on the lines in the kitchen. The washing was done and we had gone through several chapters. Mercy made us some tea and a small lunch.

In the afternoon I helped her dust the parlor and sweep the floors. We were done quickly, so we could read again. At the end of another chapter I closed the book. She leaned back in her chair and sighed. "It's ever so beautiful. He treats her like a queen."

"I don't know. He treats her like she's made of china, and she doesn't seem to have much spine to her."

"What do you know?" She was back to being cross with me. "You don't have much of a spine neither, if it comes to that," she sniffed her nose in a haughty way.

I was hurt by what she said. But, I knew it to be true. I wasn't much of a man, not like Lem and Uncle Amos. "No I don't suppose I do, but if you're gonna be mean I won't read anymore."

We both sat there in our chairs being angry at each other. I looked out the window and waited for her to say sorry. I suppose she was waiting for the same thing, but she could wait until all the oil wells ran dry before I'd apologize. Finally, I couldn't take the silence no more.

"Why does she always swoon? 'Oh, help me.'" I stood up and pretended to faint using a high voice, like I was the heroine.

Mercy threw a cushion at me, almost knocking me over. She caught me unawares. I picked it up off of the floor and threw it back at her. I then lunged out of my chair and started to punch her. She was hitting back as good as she got. We didn't hear the door open and the men come home. Uncle Amos yelled from the hallway.

"Enough, you two!"

Mercy's face was red and she turned away from me then. She left the room, edging her way by Lemuel who was laughing in the doorway. He moved a little for her. She went to the kitchen and must have put on her coat because the back door slammed, and she was gone. By then Uncle Amos was in the parlor talking to me.

"What was that all about?" he asked. "Not a very gentlemanly way to behave. You surprise me sometimes, Titus. I thought you were more sensible than that." Uncle Amos saw the book lying on the couch and picked it up. "Whose is this?"

"Mercy's," I mumbled.

"Didn't know she could read that well."

"She can't. That was my job, reading it to her so she could do her work."

"Didn't look like reading to me," Lem guffawed. "She was getting the upper hand too. Good thing we rescued you."

Uncle Amos's eyes twinkled, though his face was stern. "It's no laughing matter when a gentleman raises his hand against a woman."

"She's a girl and I'm a boy," I argued hotly. "She's a stupid, bossy girl."

"Girls and boys grow up," Uncle Amos was more thoughtful now. "Sit down, Titus. Your fists are not meant to be used against the weaker sex."

"She's not weaker. She has powerful arms." My ears were still ringing from the few punches she had delivered to my head.

"Titus, enough arguing. I will not see this kind of behavior in my home again. Do you understand?"

The twinkle was gone from his eyes and I turned my head to look out the window. It's very embarrassing fighting a girl and having the girl do the winning. It's even more embarrassing when there are witnesses.

"Yes, sir," I said.

"You might find better reading material too." He tossed the book back on the couch and headed toward the kitchen to prepare supper.

"It wasn't me chose that there book," I called after him.

I always had to get the last word in. I stayed in the parlor, watching the glow of the embers in the grate. Lem came in a little later and got the fire going again. The flames kept me company until it was time to eat.

CHAPTER
18

It was on a Saturday morning when the knock came on the front door. Uncle Amos must have been up already because he answered it straight away. I heard the murmur of voices and pressed my ear to the grate in the floor hoping to hear better. I couldn't make any sense of it. I only heard the name of Adam McCabe, and that was all.

I stopped to put on socks because the floor was freezing and I struggled into my pants. The water in the ewer was cold but I splashed it on my face anyways. I pulled on a sweater over my shirt and lifted my suspenders over my shoulders. I reached the bottom of the stairs just as Uncle Amos closed the door. He turned to me with a very sad expression on his face. I knew something very important and awful had happened.

It seems Mr. McCabe went down into his well to clear something out of it when he was overcome by the fumes. He died right next to his well after his workmen pulled him out. Uncle Amos and Mr. McCabe were good friends. My uncle would miss him.

Uncle Amos put on his coat. "I'll be gone for awhile."

The cold of the morning entered the house when he opened the door. I looked up at my big brother. I could see he wanted to go too, but thought he needed to stay with me here.

"Let's go," I suggested hopefully. "Let's go see what happened."

For once Lem agreed with me. We each grabbed a piece of bread from the pantry and ate it quickly. Our coats were on before you could say "Jack Robinson" and off we went in the direction of McCabe's well. When we got there they had already loaded the body on a wagon and covered it with a tarp. I was very disappointed. My one chance to see a dead man, and I couldn't. I thought about going to the wagon when no one was looking, lifting the tarp, and taking a peek. I wondered if people looked different when they were dead.

I sidled over to the wagon. Uncle Amos was standing there, and I pretended I just wanted to be near him. He laid his hand on my head and looked down at me for a second. His eyes were different somehow, as if he was thinking about being somewhere else. They were red around the edges like he'd been crying, but I knew that a big grown man like him didn't cry.

I was busy thinking about crying myself, when the creak of the wagon wheels made me realize it was too late for that peek. Uncle Amos was talking with the other men about funeral plans as the wagon passed with its burden.

"The preacher won't be here until next week, I believe," he said.

"Naw, he's here tomorra," a man said.

"You sure?" Uncle Amos raised his eyes.

"Sure as the sun's gonna rise."

"Titus can you run on down to Isabelle's and bring her back up to the house?"

"You mean Mrs. Ryan?" I asked all innocent-like.

"Yes, I do," was all the reply I got.

Uncle Amos followed the men, who followed the wagon back to town. I watched that sad line of folks. Most of them had taken their hats off in memory of Mr. McCabe. The wagon wheels creaked like they was crying.

I turned and ran as fast as I could to Mrs. Ryan's house. I looked in the window before knocking on the pane of glass. She was busy at the table writing figures in a big ledger. Her head came up and she spotted me at the window. I gave her my biggest smile then remembered what I had come for. She curved her finger at me to come in, so I did. She got up from the table and poured two cups of coffee.

"I don't suppose you should be drinking coffee, but we'll make allowances this time."

I was happy to get something hot to drink because it was cold out there in that blustery wind. The slush had seeped through my boots and my feet were wet. I left a trail of sock prints behind me on the kitchen floor.

"What brings you out on this miserable morning?" she asked. She knew I wouldn't be here so early except for something important.

"Uncle Amos." I paused to sip some tea. "Uncle Amos asked me to come and get you so I can take you home with me."

"Mercy is sick and can't cook?" Her eyes crinkled when she smiled.

"No, ma'am. There's been a death."

"Someone else has succumbed to the plague that's besetting this town?"

"No, ma'am. It seems Mr. McCabe succumbed to the vapors of his well."

She didn't say anything for a minute or two. I think I surprised her with that.

"Adam McCabe?"

I nodded.

"Well. . . . Well . . . that's a real tragedy, Titus. He was a respected member of this community, a beacon of light."

"Yes ma'am," I said though I didn't rightly know what she was talking about.

We each sat there sipping our coffee while waiting for the other to say something, so the loss of another life wouldn't weigh us down so. I drained the last little bit out of my cup.

"I suppose we should go." Mrs. Ryan got up, untied her apron, and put on her winter cape and muffler. "Come on then, Titus."

I put on my coat too, and the wet shoes. I looked forward to getting home and changing my socks. I opened the door for her, remembering to be a gentleman for once.

Mrs. Ryan walks very quickly. I had to run a little to keep up with her. It was like she didn't remember I was even with her. We got home soon enough but Uncle Amos or Lemuel weren't there.

"He told me to bring you here," I shrugged my shoulders. "Do you suppose he went to Mr. Whelan's?"

"Probably. I suppose they'll be hungry when they return. Come let's prepare something."

I followed her into the kitchen and helped her to make the midday meal. I don't know where Mercy was. I guess it was her day off.

It was awhile before Uncle Amos and Lemuel came back. We sat down to eat and Mrs. Ryan stayed with us. After lunch I was told to wash the dishes while she and Uncle Amos went into the parlor. Lemuel left to do something. I could hear voices and was tempted to put my ear against the door but thought I had better use my time finishing up the dishes and cleaning the kitchen.

They were still in the parlor when I was done, but I couldn't hear any more talking. I tiptoed to the door and leaned my ear against the wood but I still couldn't hear nothing. I was about to find something else to do when the door opened, and I almost fell into the room.

I could see my uncle lying on the couch, his head turned away from me. Mrs. Ryan pushed me out of the room and closed the door behind her.

"Now, Titus, did anyone ever tell you it is terribly impertinent to be listening at doors?"

"Yes ma'am," I replied.

"Then why did you do it?"

"Well, I was sorely tempted when you all were talking, but I finished the dishes anyway. Then I couldn't stop myself from trying to figure out what was going on."

"Your uncle is distraught. He has lost a very good friend. If you must know, he is weeping."

I could feel my eyes opening wider, "Uncle Amos is crying?"

"Yes," she said sharply. "Now, I want you to run down to the store for black ribbon. We'll need to make arm and hat bands. The family will be in mourning."

"Me too?" I asked.

"Yes, you too. Now run along."

"I would ma'am, but I don't have any money."

She went back into the parlor closing the door firmly behind her once again.

I stood patiently waiting in the hall for Mrs. Ryan. She came out in a few minutes and pressed some money into my hand. We didn't say anything to each other. She seemed disappointed in me and I felt ashamed. I dressed myself warmly and left.

CHAPTER

19

A group of men were huddled around the wood-stove at the back of the store talking about Adam McCabe. I walked to the dry goods counter where Mrs. Miller was waiting on a few people ahead of me. Seems they were buying black ribbon too. I hoped there would be enough for me when my turn came around.

There was. I ordered what Isabelle had told me to and left the store. Moses was up ahead at the blacksmith's, sitting on his father's wagon, just waiting.

"Hey!" His eyes lit up when he saw me. "You want to come with us?"

"I'm not sure," I replied. "Uncle Amos is up at the house and I got to get back with this black ribbon." I held the paper-wrapped package for him to see. "I suppose you heard about Mr. McCabe?"

"Yes, it was plum awful. We was working there when it happened."

"Did you see him dead?" I asked.

"Yes, and it weren't a pleasant sight."

"What'd he look like?"

"Dead."

I rolled my eyes. "Really, what did he look like?"

"He was pale and his eyes were open, staring at nothing."

"Did he die while you were looking at him then?"

"No. I couldn't get anywhere near him when he was dying. There was a whole bunch of men around him, trying to help."

"It must've been something awful."

"Yes it surely was. My father says that another good man was lost to this infernal oil."

"Uncle Amos said he was a man of integrity. They were good friends. Can I tell you something and you promise not to tell anyone?"

I got up on the wagon next to Moses.

"I saw my uncle cry," I said and waited for Moses's response.

He just sat there quiet then said, "Titus, men cry too."

I didn't want to seem ignorant so I said, "I know." Then I didn't want to lie so I said, "I didn't really see him cry, but someone told me."

Moses's daddy came out of the blacksmith shop and got on the wagon.

"Morning, Titus," he tipped his hat.

"Morning Mr. Croucher, sir," I replied.

"Coming with us, then?" he asked, noticing I hadn't got off of the wagon.

"No sir. I need to get home." I jumped down, and we promised to meet the next day at the funeral. As it happened, the whole town turned up.

At home, I found my uncle slumped on the couch. A large bottle of whiskey sat on the side table next to him. I woke him up, then I sat next to him. I put my arms around him and laid my head on his shoulder.

"It will be all right, Uncle Amos, I promise," I said, though I really didn't know how it would be. "We're here, Lemuel, me, and Mrs. Ryan."

His tears dropped down the back of my neck, and I didn't dare move, or he would know I'd seen him cry. I waited it out until his chest stopped heaving, and he was breathing normal again. He tried to talk, but his words were slurred and he didn't make much sense.

"Come on, Uncle Amos, let me get you to bed," I said.

I helped him up, and he put his arm around my shoulder. He weighed heavily down on me. We moved like that to the staircase. It was pretty hard getting to the top, but we managed, though we stumbled a few times before we made it all the way.

When we were standing next to his bed I pushed him gently, and he flopped down. I knelt on the floor to take off his shoes, and then I pulled the blankets up and made sure he was covered because it was very cold. The wind was rattling the new windows. I stood beside the bed and waited until Uncle Amos fell asleep.

Back in my room I slept like the dead, I was that tired. Lemuel was the one who got us up in the morning by frying side bacon. The smell had both of us awake and at the table.

The church was small and crowded because everyone had come to say good-bye to Mr. McCabe. We sat on the hard pews while the woodstove tried to warm up the space. The smell of damp wool and unwashed bodies was all around me. I kept on glancing over at Uncle Amos, to see if he was all right. He was pale. His face was still in the thin winter light that leaked through the windows.

The minister, who had just ridden into town the night before, read from the Gaelic Bible because it was the kind that McCabe quoted from regularly.

The sun suddenly came from behind a cloud and shone mightily on the minister's hair. He read from the Book of Job, the 29th chapter. Afterwards, Uncle Amos told me it was bout Job wishing God was back with him, lighting his life up. He talked of the river of oil coming from the rocks.

Though the words were like music, I didn't understand them. Uncle Amos explained them to me.

"The minister tried to make sense of it all," he said. "He tried to tie Adam's life and death in with the discovery of oil."

"Was that good, Uncle Amos?" I asked.

"Yes, much better than dust to dust, ashes to ashes," he replied.

You might wonder why I'm even telling you about the funeral. Well sir, it's like this. I'm telling you about this here funeral because that was the first time I saw

John and Max since they'd disappeared before Christmas. There was still mushy snow on the ground and the streets were partly thawed. Oil ran down the ruts made by the wagon wheels. The stink of oil, mixed with thawing manure was strong after the cold of winter had kept the smell in hibernation, just like the skunks.

Once the service was done, the crowd followed the minister behind the hearse to the cemetery. The sucking sounds of boots in mud and the piercing cold wind was enough to make anyone miserable. Uncle Amos looked like a sleepwalker. Every once in awhile he would stumble, but Lemuel was on his other side to hold him up.

The minister held his black hat in his hand so it wouldn't blow away. His hair stood up straight, and to my mind he looked like a stork. His long legs led us all straight to the cemetery.

Adam's wife had come in from London by the train the night before. I couldn't see her face on account of her veil, but I imagined her the way she looked that day by the creek. Everyone knew she wanted Adam to move back home and manage the store he'd left behind in the care of his brother. She had refused to set foot in our town once she left.

The story around town was that Adam had asked her to stay in Oil Springs, but she'd said, "Over my dead body." Well, she was finally here, but it wasn't *her* dead body that brought her. It was right sad to think of those words and how she must regret them.

My mind wandered the whole time we were in the procession. The wind was bitter even though the drip of snow melting from the trees was all around us. We came to the cemetery, a clearing in the bush and stopped at the newly dug grave. Had Mr. McCabe died a few weeks earlier we would not have been able to bury him right away, the ground would have been frozen hard like rock.

The minister read again from the Book of Job, something about God's light guiding us through the darkness. His voice was deep and solemn.

"Is it dark where he's going?" I whispered to Mrs. Ryan, who stood on the other side of me. She supposed it was, though she told me to be still and ask questions once we were back home.

Then something happened that I don't think any of us expected. Mrs. McCabe collapsed in a heap right at the foot of her husband's grave. The minister was holding the Bible so he couldn't help, and a man standing close by was too late in catching her. She was lucky not to hit her head on the ground.

Adam's brother, the one who minds the store, bent down and lifted her up. The minister gave his Bible to someone and helped in taking Mrs. McCabe back to the hearse. We all followed, like a herd of sheep.

Once she was seated and looking a mite better, the minister headed back to the gravesite. We all followed again excepting Mrs. McCabe and Mr. Cyrus McCabe. It was then I noticed Max McQuarrie and John Longville. They were standing off to the side. The colored folks were at the cemetery too, those who could get the time off work. You could feel the tension, it was that strong.

I went and stood next to Moses and his family while the gravediggers shoveled dirt onto the coffin. That's when John and Max walked up to us.

"You'll be sorry you ever set foot in Oil Springs," he threatened. I wasn't quite sure then if he was speaking to the Crouchers or me. But those were his words. I'll swear that on the Bible.

CHAPTER

20

That March was cold and miserable. People were tired of winter and bad tempers took a hold of the townsfolk. They complained about the weather, they complained about the mud, but mostly – thanks to John Longville, I suspect – they complained about the blacks working for less pay than the whites and stealing jobs away.

Uncle Amos came home one day very angry and upset. Mrs. Ryan was with him. It was starting to get natural, seeing those two together. Uncle Amos's shoulders were stiff with anger and I didn't even dare ask him what was wrong.

He was awfully tired these days because there was another outbreak of cholera, and the beds were full up at our house. I was told to stay out of the hospital parlor even though Mercy was allowed in. She was constantly washing and scrubbing the sick room. I didn't envy her for that.

A couple of times I leaned forward in my seat, at the kitchen table to see what was going on while Uncle Amos checked his patients. Mrs. Ryan caught me at it and smiled but shook her head just in case I was thinking of going in to them. Uncle Amos was talking about John and Max and how they were upstarts and dissatisfied souls who could do great damage in our community.

Oil Springs had one constable, and that was enough because people here treated each other pretty well most of the time. But what Uncle Amos was saying scared me. According to him, people were talking of driving the blacks out of town because of their lower wages.

"They already live outside of town," I called out. I couldn't help myself. I wanted to be part of the conversation because I cared about Moses Croucher and his family. I had spent enough time on Crooked Line to get to know most of their neighbors and they were decent enough folks. I got out of my seat and peeked around the corner of the door.

"Come in then," Uncle Amos sighed and shook his head.

"What do you mean, Uncle Amos?"

"Exactly what I said, boyo. They want to drive the Negroes out of town and far away from here."

"But . . . don't they have a right to live here too?" I asked.

"Yes, of course they do."

Uncle Amos was staring at the carpet in front of him.

"That's why they came here, right?" I had gotten farther into the room. "That's why we came too, right?"

"What?"

"To be free. We all came here to be free," I insisted.

Uncle Amos reached out to me and pulled me closer to him. "You have the right of it, Titus. They came to be free. So did we. But not everyone sees it that way. People like John Longville and Max McQuarrie think we should drive them back into the United States of America, send them 'home.'"

"But they'd be caught and made to be slaves again!"

"You're right. We can't let loudmouths like Longville control this town. We're all better than that." With those words, Uncle Amos left the parlor, grabbed his coat, and stomped out of the house. Mrs. Ryan stayed back with me. I don't think she knew whether to follow him or not.

"It's my night to cook supper," I said. "You could help, if you want, and then stay to eat."

"That's kind of you to offer," she said as she wrapped a scarf around her neck. "But I have things that need to be done. Tell your uncle I'll see him tomorrow at church."

I watched Mrs. Ryan walk away until she disappeared from sight. I really didn't want to make supper, but it was my turn. I was peeling potatoes when Lem came home. He was full of the news downtown. Seemed there was some colored man that had pushed Mrs. Mabee off of the sidewalk into the muck.

"Did you see it happen?" I asked.

"No, but McQuarrie said it did," he replied.

I told you Lem wasn't the smartest man alive. Even I knew better than to believe McQuarrie. Uncle Amos had called him and John braggarts so why would anyone believe them now?

I waited impatiently for Uncle Amos to return, but he didn't come back until real late. Lem told him what he'd heard downtown. I could see Uncle Amos was downright worried. "Seems they're using the oldest trick in the book," he said.

"What's that?" I asked.

"When you can't get people riled enough over what's really the issue, you make them believe their womenfolk are being threatened. Every man will come to the aid of their womenfolk."

ANN TOWELL

As we sat down to eat our supper, there came a loud, persistent banging on the front door. Lem answered it, and there was Righteous Freeman, one of the Negroes who lived on Crooked Line.

"You gotta come quick, Amos," he pleaded. "It's Randall Croucher's baby. He's took real bad with the croup."

Uncle Amos rose from the table. "We'll wrap him up good and bring him here. Lem, you get the horse and buggy set up. Titus, you go and get Mrs. Ryan real quick." I ran as fast as my legs could carry me and explained to her that Uncle Amos needed her something bad. There were too many sick people in our house for two people to look after. I couldn't think of anyone else to help Mercy or my uncle.

We saw quite a crowd of men walking down the street together, carrying pitch torches. When I stopped to watch them, Mrs. Ryan pulled me along and said it wasn't any of my business. Well sir, if it wasn't mine, then whose was it? I think it was all of our business because we're a community. I was starting to put two and two together by the time we reached the house.

Another crowd of men passed by, heading toward the center of town. I wanted to go see what was happening, but right then Uncle Amos came back with Mrs.

Croucher, the baby, and Beulah. Moses wasn't with them, since he and his daddy were still working at one of the sites.

The baby was crying and fretting something terrible. Mrs. Croucher was crying too, but quietly, the way grown-ups do. Tears ran down her face like rain on a window.

Uncle Amos took baby Ogden out of Mrs. Croucher's arms, handed him to Mrs. Ryan, and immediately took the kettle off of the stove. He put it on the tabletop and told her to sit next to it, then he covered them with a blanket. The steam from the kettle was supposed to help Ogden breathe.

Uncle Amos mixed a mustard plaster, while poor Mrs. Croucher paced the floor, praying. Uncle Amos gave a spoonful of medicine to the baby, who spluttered, but swallowed most of it.

After a while, Ogden settled a bit and was breathing easier, so Mrs. Ryan gave him back to Mrs. Croucher who took a turn with him. Mrs. Ryan put some more water on to boil, so they could help Ogden again later.

I got wondering about those men. They had been carrying torches and looked set on where they were going. I asked Uncle Amos if he knew anything about it, but he gave me such a stern look, I knew enough to keep quiet. Mrs. Croucher, Beulah, and the baby went into the hospital parlor so they all could get some rest.

Mrs. Croucher sang to her baby and Beulah sat on the floor, resting her head against her mama's knee. Mrs. Croucher would run her hand over Beulah's head, then touch the baby's cheek. Back and forth her hand went, as if she was caressing the greatest treasures on earth. My heart ached a little, 'cause right then I thought of my own mother. That's when Lem came home and took Uncle Amos into the dining parlor, shutting the door behind them.

I was having trouble eavesdropping until Lem cried out, "I tell you they're planning on going to the shanty town to cause trouble!"

"Where's Constable Puddicombe?" Uncle Amos demanded.

I'd had enough of listening at doors. All this had something to do with Moses and his family, and I needed to know how I could help them.

"Uncle Amos," I burst in, before they could say anything. "I need to know what's happening. I'm scared."

Uncle Amos motioned for me to close the door behind me. "Keep your voice down, son," he said. "We don't want to worry the women unnecessarily."

"The constable was trying to talk some sense into them when I left." Lem continued.

"What can I do?" I blurted out.

"You can stay here and behave," Uncle Amos said sternly.

He started walking toward the hallway. I knew he and Lemuel would be out of the house in seconds. I grabbed my uncle's arm.

"Uncle Amos, please! I need to go with you."

He shrugged off my arm and continued walking. I grabbed at him again. He stared down at me as if I was a pesky fly.

Lemuel took me aside. "Come on Titus, what do you think you can do besides getting in the way? That's a dangerous crowd out there, and we'll lose track of you. Be thoughtful for once, and stay here. Isabelle may need you for something. What can you do against an army of men?"

That's the most Lemuel had ever said at one time. I suppose you think I should have listened to him, since he put so much effort into talking. Well, I watched them leave the house. I stood there, staring out the window tears of frustration rolling down my face, and I was filled with anger. Then without another thought I went to Mrs. Ryan. "I'm not feeling well," I told her. "I think I'll lie down for awhile." "You don't seem to be hot," she said with a puzzled look on her face. I looked at the ground. "Well, it's not so much that I'm sick, as I'm tired." But I couldn't look her in the eye because I was lying.

"I guess we're all a little tired." Mrs. Ryan sighed as I pretended to head for my room.

In the hallway, I grabbed my coat from the hook on the wall and while the women were busy with the baby, I slipped into the night.

You got to believe me when I say that this is the first time I openly defied my uncle and went against his wishes.

CHAPTER

21

I crouched under the front windows and only straightened up once I was well away from the house. Then I began to run. Up ahead the torches the men were carrying glowed and flickered. There was a lot of yelling and carrying on.

A few of the better men in town were trying to talk over the hubbub. I inched my way through the crowd. For once, I was thankful to be small. I nudged and pushed through the throng of big men, but I got an elbow in the head and my glasses were knocked off. Someone stepped back on one of the lenses. I heard the sickening crunch. All I could think of was that I would be in big trouble when I showed my glasses to Uncle Amos. There was no one in town who could fix them for me.

I pushed the man to get him off my glasses. Finally he turned around to glare at me. When he moved his foot, I bent to grab my spectacles, but he stumbled backwards over me and into the man behind us. A fight broke out between the two. I supposed they were what Aunt Sadie would call liquored up.

I managed to squeeze past them, while they landed a few punches on each other and, clutching my glasses, moved through a blurry world. I made it to the front of the crowd and saw my uncle with some other men, trying to convince the mob to go home.

Constable Puddicombe stood silently, smacking the palm of his hand with a cudgel.

I ducked behind someone, put on my glasses, and peeked around the back of the man. I couldn't see my uncle clearly through the shattered lens, and I hoped he couldn't see me. Lemuel was at the edge of the crowd leaning against the hotel wall, and the streetlight created a halo around him.

John Longville stood in front of my Uncle Amos, looking very threatening. He said something that I couldn't hear, then he spat in my uncle's face.

John turned to us all and yelled, "Are we going to stand here all night yammering with the likes of these mealymouthed fools, or are we going to see that justice is done?"

Uncle Amos wiped the spit from his face. I wished

he would punch John right in the gob. "Justice? You call this justice?" he shouted.

Before he could say anything else, Longville turned and landed a punch on my uncle's jaw. He fell backwards and crashed his head hard on the wooden sidewalk. He was flat out cold.

Lemuel ran and knelt beside him. "Someone get a doctor!" he yelled.

Poor Lem. In his panic he forgot Uncle Amos was the only doctor around. I admit I was feeling pretty scared myself because I saw some blood trickling onto the wood.

There was silence while everyone took in what Longville had done. It looked for a minute like people would turn around and go back to wherever they called home, whether it was a hotel or a shanty. This was too much for John and Max. They had worked hard to get this crowd on their side. They weren't going to give up.

Max began shouting, "Let's get a move on boys! There's work to be done! We got to protect our town and our womenfolk. Are we cowards or men?"

Max got everyone moving toward violence again. They were even more riled up and excited than before. Simon Fish took a punch at whoever was beside him because it seemed like the thing to do. That man touched his torch to Simon's hair, which started to burn. The smell was awful. Lucky for Simon, someone wearing work gloves patted it out.

John yelled, "Who's with us?"

A loud shout rang out. "We are!"

By this time, Uncle Amos was struggling to get up. He tried once more. "Stop!" he cried. "Let's not do this thing. Go home before you regret this evening for the rest of your lives."

"Enough talk. It's time for action!" John yelled.

"Hear, hear," Max called out. "Action! We're men of action."

I guess Uncle Amos's patience had just run out. He was still unsteady on his feet, but he was winding up to punch Longville, when Lemuel pulled him back. I wish he hadn't done that. It would have been good to see Longville get what he deserved.

Mr. Shaw and Lemuel pushed Uncle Amos away from the crowd. Blood dripped down into his beard, and he dabbed at his mouth with the back of his hand. I watched them go, then I snaked my way out of the crowd and ran down to Crooked Line to warn the Crouchers and their friends.

I'm a fairly good runner. The cold air filled my lungs, causing them to hurt, but once I went a few blocks, I found my rhythm and they didn't bother me much. It was hard to see where I was going with my broken glasses. I was sort of crying because I was so mad at Lemuel. He should have hit Longville in revenge for Uncle Amos. John would have gone down like a poled ox. He wouldn't have stood a chance against Lem. What was the use of being so strong and big if you didn't stop bad people from doing wrong?

I reached the edge of town and headed down Crooked Line. I could barely see, it was such a dark night, but the snow-edged road at least kept me out of the swampy areas on either side.

All of a sudden I tripped and fell. I lay there and wondered what I was doing. *What can I do?* The thought rolled over in my mind. *What can a small person like me do? What can I do?* That was the first time I wished for a shotgun of my own. I would have scared anyone by firing it.

I got up when the sound of shouting reached me and saw light coming from another road leading to Crooked Line. I realized then that I was too late. The mob was almost upon the shantytown, and here I was, lying on the muddy earth daydreaming about shotguns. I felt such deep shame that my body burned under my coat. Though all seemed lost, I decided to try to warn

Moses anyway. Maybe I could dart behind the rows of hay stooks until I reached his home.

Then, starting at the top of my head and running down my back, my blood went from hot to ice cold. That was the moment in my life when I knew real terror. The first stook had been torched.

CHAPTER

22

The blaze stood out against the night sky. Men jumped around like black, dancing puppets. My feet were stuck in the muddy ground. I pretended it was the miry clay that held me fast, but it was my weak heart – my lack of courage. When they lit the second stook I pulled one foot out of the squelchy mud. Then the other foot came out, and I ran, screaming toward Moses's home.

I pushed my way between two men with torches. Their faces were made scarier by the torchlight. They looked like monsters, not men at all. John Longville was at the front throwing oil at the first shanty. When he touched his torch to the oil, the small house went up in flames. People ran out screaming. Some men had sticks in their hands and began chasing the black families, beating them over their heads, shoulders, and arms. I saw a woman stumble beneath a blow. Then a man came back to help her up. They both ran for the woods, holding hands.

I turned away, only to see a man, I'm sure it was McQuarrie, on top of a shanty, pouring kerosene on it. He jumped off and then threw his torch to the roof. It ignited in a huge flash and more people ran out of their home.

The mob hadn't reached the Croucher place yet. At least Beulah, Ogden, and Mrs. Croucher were safe. I prayed that Moses and his pa were not in their house. I was still headed in that direction, but Longville was there ahead of me. He had lit the corner of the house after pouring kerosene on it. The Crouchers escaped, but I saw Mr. Croucher confront Longville. Moses kept running, but Max caught up and began hitting him.

Mr. Croucher wrestled with Longville until others came to help. They beat on Mr. Croucher with their sticks too, but somehow he managed to get away and ran into the woods. I was heading for Moses to help him when Mr. Croucher came back out of the bush to rescue his son. He picked Moses's limp body up off the ground and cradled his son in his arms. I called out to them, and for an instant, Mr. Croucher's eyes met mine. The look on his face was one I will remember for the rest of my life. It had fear and desperation and disappointment and confusion – and hate – all mixed in together. His lips formed a single, soundless word: *Titus*. I didn't know if Moses was dead or alive, but I did know his daddy wondered what I was doing there. Surely he couldn't think I was part of all this.

Longville saw me standing there in a daze. He raised his cudgel above his head and walked steadily toward me. I didn't need any more warning. I turned and ran, not bothering to look back until I was halfway home.

My chest hurt from the smoke and all the running. I just had to stop. I was crying and shaking so hard I could hardly find my way. Everything was a living nightmare through the shattered lens of my glasses.

"Lost your way Titus?" A familiar voice behind me made me jump.

Tom Abrams was there, holding a pad and paper.

"What are you doing here, Tom?" There was reproach in my voice.

"The question is, what are *you* doing here, Titus. Your uncle sent me to find you when he realized you weren't home in your bed."

"Am I in big trouble?" I asked.

"I figure so."

He put his pad and paper in his coat pocket and took my arm. I let him lead me home.

Uncle Amos was in the kitchen holding chipped ice to his head.

I wanted to ask where Lemuel was, but the words wouldn't come. All I could do was cry and shake. Tom asked though, and Uncle Amos told us that Lemuel was helping the constable to arrest the hooligans.

What good will that do? I thought. *The damage is already done.*

I couldn't stop shaking, so Mercy fetched a blanket, put me on a chair, and wrapped me tight. She put some water from the kettle in a basin so I could warm my feet. I winced at the heat, but it felt good. Still, I couldn't answer when Mrs. Ryan asked where I'd been.

"Tom, what happened to him?" she demanded.

"Ah, Mrs. Ryan, it's a long story."

"Is it to do with the fire south of here?" she asked.

"She could see the light from the parlor window," Uncle Amos told Tom. "Is it what I think it is?"

My uncle was as pale as the bandage someone had wrapped around his head. Tom sat down next to him and they talked about what had happened. Tom jotted down notes for the article he intended to write for his paper. Uncle Amos was more than ready to talk, though he had to stop now and then to rest. Tom asked me questions too, but I could only shake and cry like some helpless baby.

Tom left soon after.

"Come here lad," my uncle said, patting the chair next to him. He put his arm around me and pressed tight as if to will the shakes out of me.

Mrs. Ryan watched the two of us and said, "There are two men in need of tending I see." She took off my glasses and shook her head over them.

"We'll get these fixed as soon as possible, won't we Amos." she said.

I don't remember much after that because I must have dozed off. Mrs. Ryan woke me to help me up to bed. She tried to unbutton my shirt, but I pushed her hands away. She sighed, almost said something, changed her mind, and left the room. The wail of a baby drifted up the stairs. All at once I remembered Moses and Mr. Croucher were hiding in the woods.

"Mrs. Ryan?" I called out. "Isabelle!"

She rushed back. "What is it, Titus? Are you all right?"

"The Crouchers. They're in the woods. Their house was burnt." My voice shook. "Can you send Lemuel to find them? Moses and his pa are going to be cold, so cold."

"You get to bed right away, and I'll see what I can do to find them."

I felt a burden lift off of me. Mrs. Ryan left only to return with a warmed brick, wrapped in a towel, to put at my feet. That seemed to help a little. She sat down on the bed, "I'll go out to find Lemuel right away and Constable Puddicombe. Don't you worry. We'll find them."

I was still trembling like a leaf in the wind on a fall day. She watched me struggle for a while then pushed my hair back on my forehead. Her palm was warm, and for that second the shaking stopped. When she removed her hand, it began again.

"Oh, Titus," she whispered. There were tears in her eyes, and she leaned over to kiss my cheek. "Sleep well, child, and call for me if you need anything."

I nodded to let her know I understood. Then, she blew the candle out. No flames to frighten me.

"Thank you," I whispered.

Those were the last words I spoke for a very long time.

CHAPTER

23

Whenever I closed my eyes that night, everything came back to me. If I lay with my eyes open, I was fine. I listened to the cry of the baby downstairs, that stopped and started over and over again. I heard the groans of the others, sick in our hospital. I don't know if I slept at all. All I remember is lying awake, afraid to close my eyes. But some time around dawn I must have dozed off because the next thing I knew, Lem was standing next to my bed and sunlight was coming through the windows. He looked tired and angry. I pulled the blankets up to my chin, thinking maybe he was mad at me.

"It's time to get up," he said and threw some clean clothes at me. I pulled the covers over my head. "Didn't you hear me? I said get up."

Lem told me I should stop acting like a baby, and there was work to be done. What kind of work, I wasn't sure but I *was* sure that Uncle Amos and Lem had something planned.

I pulled my pants on over my long underwear. It was another cold morning. I noticed how quiet it was. Baby Ogden wasn't crying anymore. I wondered if he had survived through the night.

Lem's heavy footsteps followed me down the stairs. I stopped at the parlor-turned-hospital door. Mrs. Croucher sat, in the room, with the baby in her arms. He was very still. She looked up at me and smiled. I went closer and reached out my finger to touch Ogden's cheek. It was warm and soft. I breathed a sigh of relief.

In the kitchen Mercy and Mrs. Ryan were bustling around heating water, making porridge, and putting bread into the oven. They must have been up all night looking after the sorry Sullivan lot and their patients.

"Are you feeling better, Titus?" Mrs. Ryan wiped her hands on the apron and felt my forehead. I nodded. "Come. Sit down and have some breakfast." She scooped the porridge into a bowl and set it in front of me.

"You're awful quiet this morning," Mrs. Ryan said, as she prepared a tray for Mrs. Croucher. Beulah had come into the kitchen and was eating across from me. I passed her the maple sugar and shrugged my shoulders at Mrs. Ryan.

"Cat got your tongue?" Mercy asked me as she wrung out her cloth. "You are never at a loss for words."

She turned her back and wiped the sink down. She then began on the sideboard. I tried once more to say something and then gave up. I threw my spoon down into the bowl of porridge, splattering the top of the table. Beulah looked up, alarmed.

Mercy turned around and yelled at me. "Watch what you're doing. There's enough to clean up as it is."

I ran up to my room with her words following me and slammed the door behind me. I flopped down on the bed and cried some more. The shakes started coming back, so I crawled under the blankets and tried to warm up.

Mrs. Ryan entered the room soon after. "What's wrong with you, Titus? All the slamming and noise is scaring the baby."

I heard Ogden's thin wail and wanted to say I was sorry, but I only turned my head and looked out the window at the dreary first day of spring.

"I'm off to school then," she said as she pulled my quilt up to my chin. "Mercy will need you to run to the apothecary and pick this up." Mrs. Ryan handed me a list Uncle Amos had written on a small scrap of paper.

The last thing I wanted to do was leave the house. I was scared John or Max would get me and hurt me too.

I started to shake even more, but I held out my hand for the paper. I didn't want to admit to her that I was afraid. She gave me the paper with a puzzled look on her face. She shook her head, turned around, and left the room. I followed her after a few seconds.

At the store groups of men were talking about the events of the night before. I tried not to listen but couldn't help it.

"I say we shouldn't have done it," one man said.

"They deserved what they got, trying to take an honest man's work from him," another said.

"They're honest men too, Bob."

"I never trusted the likes of them. Why would they work for less money unless they were dishonest?"

"That is the most ill-founded bit of logic I've ever heard. They were probably forced to work for less."

"I don't believe that for a minute. They was trying to work us out of a day's wage."

On and on it went as I stood close by. So many thoughts swirled in my head and none of them were good just yet. Mostly I was just afraid. This town that I had called home was not my town anymore. I no longer wanted to belong to it. If Aunt Sadie had come that day to tell me I was going to London with her, I would have gone gladly.

"Well they got their comeuppance and I won't shed a tear," the loudmouth said. "I was glad to be a part of it, clearing our town of riffraff and good riddance to 'em." He patted his belly and smiled.

I hadn't seen him till now, but Mr. Wakefield stepped out from behind the men, winked at me, and said, "There's a young man present and I think you should mind your manners – set an example of honesty and good will. We wouldn't want him turning into the likes of you."

"Who the heck are you to tell me how to behave in my own town? Seems to me we might chase your kind out of here too!"

"I would like to see you try." James Wakefield's voice was quiet but there was steel in it. He took a step toward the man.

"I got no bone to pick with you, brother," the man said.

He put his hands up in the air as if to keep Mr. Wakefield away from him. His voice was a little shaky. He then turned around and walked rapidly away from us.

"See that you keep it that way," Wakefield said to the man's retreating back.

He tipped his hat to me. I watched him with my mouth open; I was that surprised. He waited for me to say something, but all I could do was shake my head.

CHAPTER

24

Most of them said it was just white men protecting white women. But Mercy and I knew different because we knew John, and we knew the Crouchers and their neighbors. We would have sided with them any day against John Longville when it came to integrity.

Mercy spent the day complaining about her aunt and what had happened that night. I couldn't complain along with her, only nod my head.

"I don't know why anybody'd believe that old cow. I'm sure she stumbled into the road herself. Everyone knows how much she drinks."

But it really didn't matter much if that was the truth or not. What mattered was how people had reacted to it. Uncle Amos says most people want to believe things that confirm their own prejudices. They'd rather hang on to their narrow beliefs than accept something new.

"Change is painful, son," he told me, "especially if the change comes by having to face your own faults."

But I was thinking powerful thoughts. Let's say Mrs. Mabee *was* pushed off of the sidewalk by a black man. It still wouldn't seem right that all the colored people should suffer. And I reckon, don't you, that burning someone's home is more powerful wrong than pushing someone in the mud.

See, when I was pushed down last year at school, I didn't go burning down no one's home. I don't figure I would have got away with it. No sir! The punishment would have been something fierce – maybe even jail.

I could almost hear Aunt Sadie calling to me real clear. "Two wrongs don't make a right, no matter how you look at it."

Maybe Aunt Sadie wasn't such a bad sort after all. She was like medicine: miserable as all heck when you're swallowing the stuff, but good for you in the long run. She also was easier on the mind when she wasn't able to stick her nose in all my business.

I sat listening to Mercy while she mixed some of the medicine powder I'd brought home into the boiling water. I wanted to tell her my thoughts, but it would have been awful slow to write them all down on paper just then. Besides, she was too busy to pay me any mind.

I didn't dare sit with Mrs. Croucher in the hospital room. I didn't know if she was aware of all the goings on yet, and I was afraid she'd be able to read something in my face about it if I sat with her long enough. I took the paper that the powder had been wrapped in and wrote these words on it.

The men at the store want to chase every last Negro out of town. What if they find out Mrs. Croucher is here?

Mercy glanced over at me while she stirred, then came up behind my chair and rested her hands on my shoulders while she slowly read the note.

I wrote another question at the bottom of the paper. *Does Mrs. Croucher know what happened last night?*

"I don't rightly know what all happened myself. Can you tell me, Titus?"

I shook my head. A shiver ran through me and the shakes began again. Mercy didn't seem to have the patience for that, and went back to her mixing.

I could feel a chilly draft on my feet. Someone had opened the door. It was Lemuel, back from looking for the constable. I wrote *Mrs. Croucher should know what happened. We need to find her husband and Moses and get them all out of town.*

Lemuel came into the kitchen and stood next to Mercy while they read my paper.

"I found the constable. He's rounding up some help to arrest the men responsible for the riot." Lem paused. "Titus is right. We have to find the Crouchers and get them all out of here safely."

They're hiding in the woods, I wrote.

"What's wrong, Titus? You still not talking?"

I looked up to catch Mercy sending him an angry look. Lemuel was confused and a little irritated. I didn't blame him because he had probably seen what happened last night too, and *he* could still speak.

I began to wonder where Uncle Amos was. I supposed he might be sleeping off his concussion upstairs. I couldn't have been more wrong.

Up to now, I hadn't even thought of going into the woods to find Moses, but all of a sudden I had to know if he was alive or dead. I got my slate and wrote, *I'm going to find Moses*, and showed it to Lem.

Lem told me that I wasn't to set foot outside the house and that Uncle Amos had found many Negroes in the woods and was setting broken arms and binding wounds. Lemuel grabbed food from the pantry and loaded it into a leather satchel while he spoke. He told Mercy he would be back around suppertime and with no explanation at all, he left. Mercy had it figured out. "He's taking it to the people in the woods," she told me.

I jumped up from the chair and ran after my big brother. He was in the barn saddling the horse. I yanked at his arm and tried to choke out my warning, but the words wouldn't come.

"Slow down," Lem said. He took me over by the window and gave me a nail that was lying on the sill. "Spell it out."

Be careful. It took me a while to scrape this into the new wood, and those words can still be seen today.

"All right, Titus," Lem said. "I'll take Tom Abrams with me. We'll make sure no one sees where we're going."

I was thankful that Tom was going with him and nodded my head over and over again.

"Don't worry, Titus. I'll be back, and then we'll find a way to get Mrs. Croucher's whole family together again."

I was so thankful I hugged him and then hugged the horse's neck too! I watched from the barn door as Lem headed toward Tom's place. My teeth chattered as I headed back to the house.

"What was that all about, dashing off like a mad man?" Mercy joked when I reappeared. I felt like a mad man, that's for sure. I couldn't get the images of last night out of my head. It hurt so bad I wanted to scream.

I sat down on the stairs by the front door. I was hunched over, holding my head in my hands. Beulah came and sat beside me.

"You all right Titus?" She patted my hand. "Your head hurt?"

I shook my head no. She pointed at the broken lens of my specs.

"It's broke! Can you still see?" she asked.

I lied again and nodded. It wasn't an out-and-out lie because I could kind of see through that lens. But it made the world look all shattered and broken. The truth is, I could see everything so much clearer when my eyes were closed. I got up and walked to the door of the hospital. Ogden was sleeping now. He breathed noisily through his mouth because his nose was plugged, but he breathed, and that was the main thing. Mrs. Croucher looked up and smiled.

"He'll be fine now," she said and stroked her baby's head. "I reckon we should get on home soon," she added.

I turned away from her. She didn't have a home anymore, leastways not here in Oil Springs. There were three other patients lying in the room. Two were sound asleep while the third was propped up on pillows, reading. I supposed he would be well soon.

"There was such a commotion last night. Do you know what transpired, son?" he asked.

I only shook my head and went into the kitchen and wrote the words, *Someone has to tell Mrs. Croucher she's got no home.*

Mercy read the paper. "Oh, Titus. She knows. She means her other home."

All of a sudden, Mrs. Croucher was standing in the kitchen doorway with her shawl on. "Beulah is with the baby. I'd best go and see to the menfolk."

Mercy jumped into action. "Oh no you don't! Nothing you do is going to help them in any way. You stay put until Amos comes for you."

"Why, Miss Mercy, don't carry on so. I need to get this done. The baby, he's fine now. I be back directly."

"You will do nothing of the sort." I don't know where Mrs. Ryan came from, but there she was helping Mercy convince Mrs. Croucher to stay. "You will remain here if I have to sit on you."

I almost laughed when she said that, but this was no laughing matter.

"But I reckon my man needs me and my boy, too." Mrs. Croucher had tears in her eyes.

"How can you help them if you get hurt?" Mrs. Ryan asked. "There are angry, mean men out there, and we don't know what else they might do. Please, Mrs. Croucher, stay here until Amos comes for you."

The baby began to cry again. Mrs. Croucher got up quickly and rushed into the parlor.

"Thank goodness for that," Mrs. Ryan chimed. "Little Ogden saved the day."

Suddenly I was powerful tired and I couldn't keep my head up. I needed to sleep something fierce. My arms slipped down to the table and my head followed. That's all I knew, until I woke up to loud banging at the front door.

CHAPTER

25

"Open up Sullivan!" Someone was hollering and pounding away on the solid oak door.

I looked around me as Mrs. Ryan came into the kitchen, whispering fiercely. "Take the Crouchers up the back stair. Hide them in the attic."

Mercy handed Mrs. Croucher a rag soaked with whiskey. I wondered what she was going to do with it. I led the family up the back staircase. The Crouchers and I were real quiet and the baby just happened to be sleeping. He did rouse a bit but Mrs. Croucher put the rag to his mouth and he sucked on it, instead of fretting.

"Mama –" Beulah began, but her mother clamped a hand over her mouth.

"Sssh. Hush now, Beulah love," was all she said.

We were just climbing into the attic when we heard a rumpus downstairs. Men were yelling at the women as I pushed the Crouchers up the ladder. I climbed up too, and then reached to pull the ladder up. I was just closing the trapdoor when I heard them climbing the stairs.

They went into the bedrooms, hollering to each other. "They ain't here." "They ain't here, either."

One of them spotted the trapdoor. It sounded like John.

"They must be up there," he said.

The whiskey had worked and the baby was asleep again. Beulah was right next to me, shaking and shivering. Or maybe it was me shivering and shaking. You couldn't tell who was doing what, we were lying that close to each other.

Mrs. Croucher's fingers clutched my arm like a vise. It hurt but I didn't move. The men hollered down to Mrs. Ryan to demand a ladder.

She must not have answered because they clattered downstairs again. I opened the trapdoor a little so I could hear better. It sounded like more people had entered the house. Mrs. Ryan screamed and then there was lots of banging, like people were throwing each other against the walls.

There was a fight going on down there. I closed the door again, but the darkness was terrifying, especially for Beulah, who whimpered.

Mrs. Croucher warned her to hush up, or she would have to pinch her real good. How that was supposed to make the poor child stop crying, was beyond me, but strangely enough it worked. The poor little girl sniffled in the dark, but made no more noise than that.

Then I heard Lem yelling at Longville, calling him the scum of the earth. Then Uncle Amos chimed in, and I knew it was safe to go down. I didn't want anyone else to know that we were hiding the Crouchers, so I told them to stay put a while longer.

When I reached the main floor, Longville and McQuarrie were sitting by the front door with their hands tied. Uncle Amos told Lemuel to fetch the constable.

Longville snarled when he saw me. "I haven't forgotten you, kid. You'll get yours soon enough."

The next thing surprised me. Uncle Amos kicked him in the leg, good and hard. I had never seen him so angry. This time Longville couldn't catch him off guard.

"Mighty easy to kick a man when he's trussed up like a hog," McQuarrie said.

Longville glared daggers at my uncle. "Don't suppose you got the guts to fight me fair and square."

"Since when has *fair* been important to you, Longville? Do you suppose it was fair getting the mob riled last night and burning innocent people out of their homes?"

"They had it coming." Longville wasn't a bit sorry for what he done.

Uncle Amos hauled John to his feet, spun him around, and untied his hands.

"You want to fight fair and square?" Uncle Amos even scared me, he was that angry.

John smiled and spat in my uncle's face. Uncle Amos wiped the spittle away with his shirtsleeve. Then he hauled off and slugged Longville in the face. John went flying against the wall.

"That was for fleecing my nephew. This is for scaring his little brother." Another fist flew. John slumped to the floor, next to his buddy.

Uncle Amos was about to haul John up again, when Constable Puddicombe and Lem came through the door.

"Hold on there, Amos. 'Pears to me this fella is already beat. Let up, now."

Blood trickled from the corner of John's mouth. He'd be carrying a shiner come tomorrow. Served him right. The constable put an arm around Uncle Amos and moved him away from the men on the floor. Mrs. Ryan's face was white as a sheet. I don't suppose I ever saw her eyes that big, neither.

A few people helped to haul off the "hooligans."

That's what Aunt Sadie called them when we told her the story.

Uncle Amos leaned against the wall. I knew his head was paining him. He closed his eyes and breathed heavily. I wanted to tell him how proud I was of him, but you already know that my tongue wasn't working inside of my head. Some color had crept back into Mrs. Ryan's face. She took my uncle's arm and led him into the kitchen.

"Go and tell the Crouchers it's safe now," she told me. "They can come down."

I didn't realize it in all the excitement, but my legs had set to shaking again. I made it up the stairs, my knees knocking like a newborn calf's and fetched the Crouchers. The whiskey must have really worked because that there baby never woke even during all that noise and fighting downstairs. Beulah's eyes were like two full moons. I suppose they would grow a mite bigger when she saw she didn't have a home no more.

Mrs. Ryan gave a drink of whiskey to Uncle Amos. She offered some to Mrs. Croucher too.

"No ma'am. No thanks. I don't drink spirits, seeing all the problems it causes."

Mrs. Ryan looked ashamed, and Uncle Amos stared at his cup, then pushed it away. "I can see your point,

Mrs. Croucher," he said respectfully. "It's the drink that gives men false courage to do wrong."

"Yes sir, it does. I reckon last night's tragedy could have been stopped if there was no drinking involved."

"I reckon you may be right," Mrs. Ryan said. "Though there are some who don't need spirits to rile a mob and make trouble. No . . . some people are just born mean."

Finally, I got around to asking my uncle what happened to Moses. Of course, I wrote it down on my slate. I supposed the reason I waited so long to ask him was because I was real worried that Moses was dead, and I didn't want to know the truth. Uncle Amos told me he had set some broken bones and Moses was in very rough shape. Lem would bring them home to us under the cover of darkness.

They hid in our house for a few days, though I hardly saw them because I spent most of the time up in my room. Moses lay in my bed, recovering. We never said a word to each other. I know that must seem strange to anyone reading this, but Moses slept most of the time because of the medicine my uncle was giving him. Me, I still wasn't talking.

I watched Moses sleep while I sat in a corner of my room. All the beds were taken downstairs. It was awful difficult, seeing my friend in that state. Anger began to build in me and suddenly, I was throwing things around the room. Moses awoke and tried to sit up. The fear in his eyes was dreadful. I stopped what I was doing when I saw that fear, but it was too late.

I went to him, and he backed away from me. I was ashamed of myself then, knowing full well I had made Moses relive that night. I left the room, closing the door quietly behind me. I sent Mrs. Croucher up to look in on him.

I got some blankets and a pillow from Lem's room and banished myself to the parlor where I could hear the adults in the kitchen. It was soothing just to know they were there.

CHAPTER
26

No one knew what to do with Moses and me over the next few days. I was told it would be best to stay away from him while he healed. Uncle Amos kept the curtains closed in the house so no one would know we were hiding his family. I tried to help a bit but I was still shaky and not feeling well. When Mercy brought me soup one day, I threw it on the ground in a display of temper. I don't even know what set me off.

"Well, I never," she huffed. "You always were uppity."

She cleaned up the mess and told Uncle Amos that was the last time she was bringing me anything to eat. I could come to the kitchen and eat with the rest of them. All the while I was feeling sorry for myself, Uncle Amos, Lem, and the Crouchers were working to see that justice was done. People came and went at our house because of meetings they held in the kitchen.

They tried to get witnesses willing to testify against the men who had done this. Most of the men arrested had escaped while Constable Puddicombe and his deputies were bringing them to the small jailhouse. Baby Ogden and Moses were getting better. In a few days, they would travel back to Kent County where their real home was. Uncle Amos said Mr. Croucher was heartily sick from all that had transpired here. He was heartsore. He'd figured this was the land of freedom, but he figured wrong. At least by now he knew I'd had nothing to do with taking part in that night and that I had only tried to warn them.

Lem told me that the papers were saying the Americans who came to Oil Springs for the oil boom were responsible. They were for slavery and just hid up here to escape fighting in the war. I don't suppose I blame them none for not wanting to fight in a war. I read enough in the Blackwood's magazine about the war to know it was awful.

While everyone was busy, I stayed alone in that room reliving the horrible night over and over. At least no one was killed. Many of the black folks had left right away with their horses and wagons. They'd had enough of working for lousy wages in a dangerous village.

A few days must have gone by when Uncle Amos came to talk to me. I was holding a book in my hand but hadn't been able to read. It takes powerful concentration to read when your mind is somewhere else . . . remembering. But, it also takes a good pair of glasses.

"How you feeling boyo?"

No words came out of my mouth.

"Titus, the time is now to begin to talk. We want to have the people responsible for this tried in court."

I still said nothing.

"Do you understand?"

Nothing.

"I know you were there, as were many others, but it's the others who were part of the problem. You were a witness, and we need you, Titus, to identify the ones who started burning the homes of the colored folks."

I could see the drips of the snow melting from the roof. The sun would catch them and sparkled through them. I wanted to tell Uncle Amos to look and see how beautiful it was but I also knew he wanted me to answer questions, questions I wasn't able to answer.

"Son, I know sometimes people can't talk after something like this but I need you to talk anyways. You need to remember what you saw that night and tell me."

His voice was soft and tempting. I wanted to answer so much, I did truly, but my brain and my tongue weren't connected.

I kept staring out of the window. It was like his voice was somewhere else and not in the room. The drops of melted snow were more real to me than my uncle as he pleaded with me. I could not seem to turn to him and give him what he wanted, even though he tried very hard to reach me.

I heard him sigh. He turned my head toward him with his big hand and looked down into my eyes like he was searching for something he had lost. I guess he couldn't find anything there because he turned away and left the room. I reached my hand out after him, but I didn't have the energy to get up or call to him. I was trapped in my own body with my useless brain and my good-for-nothing tongue.

To tell you the truth, I don't rightly remember a lot from those days. It must have been the day the Crouchers were leaving back for Kent county. I think I must have held a book in my hands most of the time because when Moses knocked to come in I stared down at the book and wondered how the knocking noise could come from it. When I noticed a movement through the corner of my eye I looked up, and there was Moses.

"I hate this town and what they did to us."

I nodded. What could I say even if I could say something? I picked up my slate and wrote *I hate it too*. Then I added *I hate myself more*.

"Why?" Moses asked. "My daddy said you tried to warn us."

I wrote, *Because I couldn't stop them.*

"Listen here, Titus. Your uncle told me you couldn't talk. I figure you got hurt too, just like me, even though you're not carrying bruises."

His head still had a bandage on it and his one arm was in a sling. Uncle Amos said he had broken ribs too but there wasn't anything he could do about that.

"You can help us now," Moses said, looking at me very intently.

I wrote the word *how* followed by a very big question mark.

"We need you in court."

I wrote the words *I can't even talk, how can I help?*

"You'll be able to talk by then. Your uncle and my pa have a lawyer from Sarnia to take our case. I'm a witness too, but you have to give me the names of the people. If I describe them, can you tell me their names?"

I nodded.

Moses went on to describe John and Max and another two men who I knew to be Henry Wren and Samuel

Fish. He already knew John and Max. I wrote their names down for Moses. There were others too, but it turns out they never got charged.

Moses was excited. "That's who Lemuel thought they were when I described them."

Lemuel came in while we were talking and writing. He said that the town was quite now and most people were ashamed of their part in it all. They wished now they had tried to stop it. "Just goes to show what drink can do to a crowd."

Moses looked down and pulled at a hangnail. "It's more than that, Lem," he said. "They all were itchin' to do something long afore that."

"What are you saying?" he asked Moses.

I wanted to scream at my big brother. "Open your eyes. See what's in front of you. Didn't you hear them complain about the colored folk all the time?"

But I could only sit there, frustrated that I had lost my voice when I needed it more than ever. All those years of talking about nothing and now something needed to be said, and I couldn't say it.

CHAPTER

27

The Crouchers left in the dead of night. I heard noises down by the barn. I wiped the moisture off of the window with my sleeve, and looked out to see Lem holding a lantern. The family must have kept to the shadows because I couldn't see them. The barn door creaked open. Lem had worked out what he was going to say if anyone should ask him where he was going. He was fetching medical supplies.

I don't know how they did it, but Mr. Croucher's horse and wagon were stowed in our barn. With luck no one would look too close at the horse because it was dark brown, instead of black. All the Crouchers were hidden in the back and covered with blankets.

We had said good-bye earlier, Moses and me. We patted each other's backs and shook hands.

"Promise you'll be a witness?" he asked one more time before he left.

I nodded, though I didn't see how I could do it. That's when Uncle Amos said I should start writing things down that happened that night, and maybe I would get my voice back. He could see that I wasn't getting enough sleep because he mentioned how tired and worn out I was. He was the one that came running every time when I screamed at night. I couldn't quite figure out how I could yell in my sleep, but do nothing when I was awake.

The wheels creaked as they went down the road, heading due south, and I remember thinking how strange it was that they had to head south to safety this time, instead of following the north star or *drinking gourd*. Uncle Amos had told me about that once.

"Oh he's a veritable font of information," Aunt Sadie said last Christmas, when I bragged to her that he had so much knowledge. I had been arguing with her that I could learn so much from Uncle Amos.

My uncle thinks I'm destined to be a lawyer. That's the word he used, *destined*. He figured a person who could talk as much as me should have no trouble being a lawyer. What he didn't figure on is lawyers have to have courage too.

Well, by now you've surely figured, I took my uncle's advice and began writing. Lem showed up one morning with some notebooks and a pen. He brought some ink and moved a table into my room.

At that point, Lem took my glasses. "These need to be fixed, Titus. You might have to leave off reading for awhile . . ."

I nodded to show him I understood. It would be nice to see a world where everything didn't look like it was in pieces. Lem put the glasses in his pocket, and told me he'd take them to Sarnia and have them repaired.

My hand is sometimes sore because there is so much I have to tell you about. I want you to know how good Moses was, and how his family never did no one any harm. I learned from Moses to be quiet some of the time. He showed me that words weigh heavy on you if you talk before you think. He figured words were more powerful if you didn't overuse them. Moses should be the lawyer, to my way of thinking. He knows when to speak and when to be quiet. He's also smart and longs for justice, more than anyone I've ever met. Even more than Uncle Amos, and that's saying a lot.

I suppose there are some who are happy I can't speak. Aunt Sadie would probably say "God has struck you dumb so you'll learn to listen."

So I listened to her voice in my head. I listened to the sounds of Mercy cleaning house, humming and singing. I listened to the sound of the anvil in the blacksmith shop. I listened to the clop of horses on the road, the creak of wheels, the sounds of men shouting hello to one another. I listened to the crackle of the wood in the grate and the spring rain against my window. I listened to the beginning of birdsong, to the opening and closing of doors, to the murmur of voices and the running of feet along the boardwalk. I listened and listened and yet, I didn't get my voice back. So I wrote and wrote, and my hand cramped. My fingers were black with ink. The first book was filled, then the second and third. I started on the fourth.

I wanted to get to the end of all this. I figured when I was done writing, I should be able to talk. Then I began to worry that I wouldn't be able to talk because my throat wasn't getting exercise. What if I had to learn to speak all over again, like a little baby?

I still woke at night and saw fire all around me, but I knew now it was a dream, and the dream didn't have the same power over me. I was thankful that Beulah and the baby hadn't had to see the burning of their home. Beulah would probably be sleeping good at night, and she would be back with family and friends. Moses was probably back at school, learning right quick.

I was almost at the end of this book when Uncle Amos came up to see me. He said the court date was set for May 15, only a week off. I felt a frantic need to finish this book because I had decided to act as a witness. And sir, if my voice didn't work, I sure hoped you would believe the words of two boys over the words of grown men, even if you had to take the time to read most of mine. Writing these here books was something I needed to do. If Moses had the courage to speak out I would too. If my voice fails me, maybe these words won't.

I figured I had to get ready for the court day somehow, so I started coming out of my room and helped with chores around the house. I still didn't have the courage to go to the store or post office, but I tried leaving the yard once and broke out in a cold sweat. My legs were shaky and I felt like I was going to vomit.

I returned to the house where Mercy was ironing some shirts for us to wear the next day. She looked up at me and raised her eyebrows.

I shrugged my shoulders and lifted my palms in the air as if asking her what? She smiled and continued to iron. There was something secretive about her as if she wanted to keep something from me. I wondered what it was, but felt too queasy to stay in the kitchen long. I went up the stairs and began writing again. I could see where this was doing me some good because each day I slept a little better and today I finally had left the gate and stood in the road way out where the manure was steaming and the oil ran in little rivulets through the dried ruts in the road.

I was real nervous about the court date. I heard Lem and Uncle Amos talk about it with Mrs. Ryan and Tom Abrams. Tom was going to be there to cover it for the paper. There were only two still being held in custody. The rest had either escaped or been let go. Uncle Amos said that justice was not always served and often judges were afraid of the people too.

"I'd like to believe that most people will be on our side of things, Titus, but then I never thought something like this could ever happen in Oil Springs," Uncle Amos said.

He took my pulse, felt my brow, did all the things that he normally did when he checked up on me. He also looked carefully at my eyes each time.

"It was only a handful of people, Amos," Mrs. Ryan's voice was soft.

"You call a hundred people or more a handful?" Uncle Amos yelled.

That was the first time I saw him angry with Mrs. Ryan, and I didn't like it. There was enough anger already in this town. I could feel it through the walls of the house. When Lem and Uncle Amos came home I could see it in the tension of their shoulders. I could hear it in their voices when they talked about it. All we could do was wait and see what the day in court would bring.

I was glad that all the colored families had left because I wasn't sure what could happen after the court date. The last thing I wanted was to see another riot.

The evening before the court case, Tom came and had supper with us. Mrs. Ryan and Mercy were there too. We were very quiet and ate without much talking. I think everyone was nervous. I pushed my plate away after a few mouthfuls.

"Titus is feeling like the rest of us," Uncle Amos said with a crooked smile. "I don't feel hungry, either."

Mercy moved her plate away too. "Don't like your own cooking?" Tom teased her.

"She cooks well enough," Lem muttered in between mouthfuls. I don't think there is anything that would keep my brother from food. We all watched him as if he had sprouted two heads. But really, he was the only sensible one of the lot. Starving to death wasn't going to do any of us much good.

Tom pulled something out of his pocket and glanced at Uncle Amos, who nodded. He handed the package to me. It was small and oblong. I unwrapped it to find a black case. Inside were my fixed glasses. I put them on. It was startling to see everything so clear once again.

My smile of gratitude must have been very wide because everyone at the table had these foolish grins on their faces. Slowly but surely, my life was returning to normal. Having my glasses back was another step in the right direction.

CHAPTER
28

I t was May 14, the night before the trial. I still had no voice, and where was I going to get one? I don't believe in miracles, though Mercy says they happen all the time.

Mrs. Ryan looked at me worried, while Uncle Amos kept rubbing my head as if that would help me. I figured he'd probably rub the hair right off of my skull, and I would be the sorriest looking witness ever.

What I didn't know was that Mrs. Ryan and my Aunt Sadie had been writing letters to each other through all this. Mrs. Ryan let her know about the happenings in our town. And so it came about that Aunt Sadie decided to take the train down to Wyoming. She got a ride on the stage to Oil Springs and ended up on our verandah late that night. She told us the bumps in the road were so bad that the passengers were often thrown from their seats into the floor of the coach. There were mostly men in the coach and she was indignant that she had to suffer like that. It was immodest and improper to be lumped together with a bunch of people, banging into one another.

Uncle Amos, Lem, and me glanced at each other while she was complaining. It was a great matter for us not to laugh. Uncle Amos gave me a stern eye when he saw my mouth curve into a smile. But there was a twinkle in that eye. I supposed we would have a good laugh over it when Aunt Sadie was gone.

She ordered us to carry her luggage to the guest room, and we all did what we were told because we wanted Aunt Sadie to leave here a happy woman this time. I was glad she had come to see me in court. It meant she loved me, didn't it? Or did it mean she hadn't given up on the idea of taking me back to London with her?

Either way, I wanted her to be happy she had come to see me. I overheard her talking with Uncle Amos in the hallway, while I was cleaning myself up for bed.

"I don't know what you are thinking, letting that boy go on the witness stand tomorrow," she said.

I suppose she thought I was asleep already. My hands paused over the ewer basin as I strained to hear. I tiptoed to the door, dripping water as I went.

Uncle Amos didn't respond because I don't think he knew what to say. Besides, Aunt Sadie didn't give him much opportunity to speak.

"He's lost his voice, in case you haven't noticed." I felt sorry for my uncle. "What do you think he can do up there in his condition, that would be any use to anyone? Hasn't he been terrified enough? I think he should stay here . . ."

Her voice droned on, and I pictured Uncle Amos, standing there with his head hanging. I wanted to call out to him to speak up, but he remained silent. Aunt Sadie carried on something terrible. Where was my uncle's tongue? Where was his courage? I could feel the blood boiling in my veins and I wiped my hands on my trousers. I ran into the hallway.

"You shut up! What do you know?" I shouted.

Aunt Sadie turned to me, her eyes glowing like a cat's in the dark.

Then I woke up. I'd heard myself yell, hadn't I? Or had I? I lay there for a few seconds before Lem ran into my room.

"What's going on, Titus?" he asked.

He held a candle high over me to get a good look. "Did you just holler?" Uncle Amos and Aunt Sadie were next in the room.

"What was that all about?" Aunt Sadie looked frightened.

I pictured her glowing eyes from the dream and felt angry again. Uncle Amos sat down on the bed.

"I suppose you're all worried about the morning," he remarked. "Look, Titus, we were wrong to have you agree to be a witness. Tomorrow I'll tell the attorney that you won't be able to do this."

"Aren't there any others who will come forward?" Aunt Sadie asked.

"No. Looks like there are those willing to lie for the likes of them, though," Uncle Amos replied. "Do you think I wanted to put Titus through this? If I could have found someone else, I would have. People just don't want to get involved. They figured all the colored folks are gone, and now, we can get back to living in peace with each other."

The conversation went on over my head. They talked sadly as if it would all be over because most of the witnesses were from the black community. Uncle Amos, Lem, and me were the rare white folks willing to put our feet forward to help them. It was depressing to see my family get more and more despondent as they talked.

We had been more hopeful at dinner and so anxious we couldn't eat. Now we were hang-dog and I didn't like it one bit. I thought I would try one more time to speak.

So, I opened my mouth and said, "I can do it."

No one noticed me. They just carried on talking – kind of arguing. Lem was standing up for Uncle Amos and his voice was getting louder. It wasn't often that Lem lost his temper.

Words began flashing like swords, words that were cutting. At least it was Lem, this time, not me hurting my aunt.

Finally I had had enough.

"I CAN DO IT!" I yelled.

That stopped them in an all-fired hurry. The look of shock on their faces was enough to make me laugh. I laughed so hard tears came from my eyes, and I couldn't stop. They didn't know what to do with me. It was as if me talking now was more of a shock to them than when I lost my voice in the first place. Finally, Aunt Sadie found her tongue.

"The boy's hysterical. What should we do with him?"

"That's enough now, boyo." Uncle Amos clapped me on the back, which made me cough. But it sure stopped my laughing.

"Did you just talk, Titus?" Lem asked.

I nodded. My fingers picked at the threads on my quilt.

"I can do it." I said.

This time my voice was a little squeaky like a door that had rusty hinges from not being used in a long time. Aunt Sadie and Lem laughed first, but Uncle Amos and I joined in before long. We hugged and hooted. It felt so good to know I could speak again. It was the strangest thing, but after struggling for so long, it seemed to come easy. Suddenly, I wasn't so nervous anymore. I almost looked forward to seeing that court-room in Sarnia.

"I think we should all try to sleep," Aunt Sadie said picking up her candle. "It'll be a long day tomorrow, and the next . . ."

". . . and the next," I responded.

". . . and the next," Lem said.

". . . and the next," Uncle Amos laughed and led them out of my room.

He turned back at my door. The candle filled his face with light. I loved my uncle.

"You're a brave lad," he said.

EPILOGUE

When I entered the courtroom, John and Max were in the dock. They didn't look none too happy. When I walked past John he sneered, "Cat got your tongue?"

He must have heard about my affliction. The guard told him to keep quiet and he did after that. Max looked scared and not so full of himself, but John was defiant sitting there. He would find out soon enough that the cat had returned my tongue.

I had to put my hand on the Bible and swear to tell the whole truth and nothing but the truth so help me God. Well I tried to do just that. I trusted the judge had read all that I'd written and I said as much to him. I didn't figure I wanted to start all over at the beginning to tell him what had happened here, in Oil Springs on March 20, 1863. It's a day that's marked forever in my memory. I was there to do the right thing, to use my voice and see that justice was served. I stood beside my friend Moses who witnessed there too.

As God is my witness, all the events leading up to that fateful day are written in these books. May He strike me dead if I have told a lie. I've no more to add or subtract.

The lawyer let me step down from the witness box and I looked over at John Longville, who stared in amazement. You could see he had been counting on me being dumb. Both John and Max got a couple of years in the Kingston penitentiary. That was all.

But I stayed on in Oil Springs, and Uncle Amos eventually married Mrs. Ryan. Mercy still helps out, and Lem has stayed on, though every now and then he talks about moving. These people are my family. They are the reason I still live here, in this swamp.

ACKNOWLEDGMENTS

This is a work of fiction whose characters and circumstances are based loosely on historic events. This story would not have been written without the inspiration of my children and grandchildren; Charles Fairbank and Pat McGee, whose oil business has been in production for 150 years – walking their fields is to step back in time to where this story takes place; my friend Lawrene Denkers and my daughter Naomi, who both critiqued the original manuscript; Gwen Robinson of the Chatham Kent Black Historical Society, who gave moral support; Kathryn Cole and Kathy Lowinger, who maintained the spirit and essence of the work; and lastly my husband, Larry, who shares my life in every way.